FOLENS ENGLISH

WAYS OF SEEING

TERRY BROWN
MIKE FLEMING

This book is intended to engage students in interesting and meaningful language and literature work within realistic contexts appropriate to 11-12 year old concerns.

There are 12 units, each one about a different subject. Every unit starts with a lead-in for all students and then encourages different activities for students working at widely different attainment levels. The text is presented as a double-page spread for ease of use, and is suitable for all abilities.

(1) Core activities are highlighted by the use of coloured circles, and there are extension activities for further work.

Extra support material for all the units can be found in the accompanying Teachers' book, all of which is photocopiable.

☆ A star symbol in the text indicates that relevant material is available to support weaker students, extend the advanced ones, as extra resources or to provide further structure to the work in the text. There are other sheets, not attached to units, aiming to correct common errors.

English is presented as a unified subject in which language work arises naturally and meaningfully in context. We have included complete texts rather than extracts where possible, and drawn on accessible works from major writers of the past.

Terry Brown
Mike Fleming

© 1990 Folens Limited, on behalf of the authors.

First published 1990 by Folens Limited.

Folens Limited, Albert House, Apex Business Centre, Boscombe Road, Dunstable LU5 4RL.

ISBN 1 85276087-7

Printed and bound in Great Britain by The Eagle Press Plc, Blantyre

Contents

What would it feel like to grow smaller instead of bigger? The world would become a very different place. This unit is about being - or feeling - small in a large person's world.

Imagine that you wake up one morning. You find you cannot quite reach the alarm clock to turn it off. Your pyjamas seem to be too big for you. You get dressed and your clothes feel baggy. You look into the mirror but you can only see the top of your head. Can you actually be shrinking? In the following story Steven realises that he is shrinking after he has arrived at school.

It was Steven's first day at his new secondary school. He was feeling nervous. As he approached the main gate he was reminded of his first day at infant school seven years ago. Everything had gone wrong. He had arrived late because the dog had chewed a hole in his new trousers and he had to wait to get them mended. At morning break a girl called Samantha had bitten him because he had stood on her toe, and in the afternoon he had wet himself because he had been too frightened to ask to go to the toilet. Surely today could not be that bad.

He went into the yard and looked around for someone he knew. It was easy to tell who the new first years were because they were the only ones wearing new blazers. He hoped that nobody would notice that he was wearing his brother's old blazer. His mum could not afford a new one and she had insisted that he wear his brother's.

"That kid's wearing his dad's jacket."

Steven did not turn round to see where the voice came from but sped around a corner of the building out of sight. Surely it wasn't that obvious? The blazer had only been worn a few times by his brother and it was quite a good fit. Or rather, it had been quite a good fit when he had first tried it on. He looked down at the sleeves and realised that right now they came several inches over the end of his hands. Not only that but his trousers were starting to feel all baggy and bunched up at the knees, and the bag which he was carrying was starting to scrape along the ground. He was shrinking. There was no other explanation. He saw Jenny, a girl from his

junior school coming towards him. He liked her and she quite liked him, or so he thought. She walked past without seeing him. It was not surprising. He realised as she passed by that he only came up to her waist.

His clothes were now starting to look ridiculous. He was shrinking rapidly and he needed to tell someone.

A teacher in the yard was starting to organise the new first years into their classes. He walked over.

"Name."

"Please sir, Steven Westlake and I'm shrinking."

"You are in class 1T. Miss Hodgson will be your form teacher. I'm sure you'll get on well with her."

"Sir, I think I'm shrinking."

"You will get your timetable from your form teacher and there will be a short assembly before break. If you have any problems let me know."

"I'm shrinking."

"What's that? Shrinking? Do you have a note from your parents to say you're shrinking?"

"No Sir."

"Then you can't be, can you? Hurry along now, Miss Hodgson will be waiting for you."

 The above story was written after reading *"The Shrinking of Treehorn"* by Florence Parry Heide. You might like to look for the book in the library and read the story yourself.

 Imagine that Steven goes to see the Headteacher to explain what is happening to him. In pairs write out the conversation which they had.

Imagine that you start shrinking and you end up less than two inches high. The world would look very different to you: a bowl of water would be a vast ocean in which to swim, an insect would become a hideous monster, a flower-bed would become a huge jungle, full of dangers. Think of some other examples of how life would be different if you suddenly became tiny.

Look at the photographs below. They are close-ups of everyday objects, the way they might look if you were very small. Can you say what they are? (The answers are on page 96.)

A

B

C

D

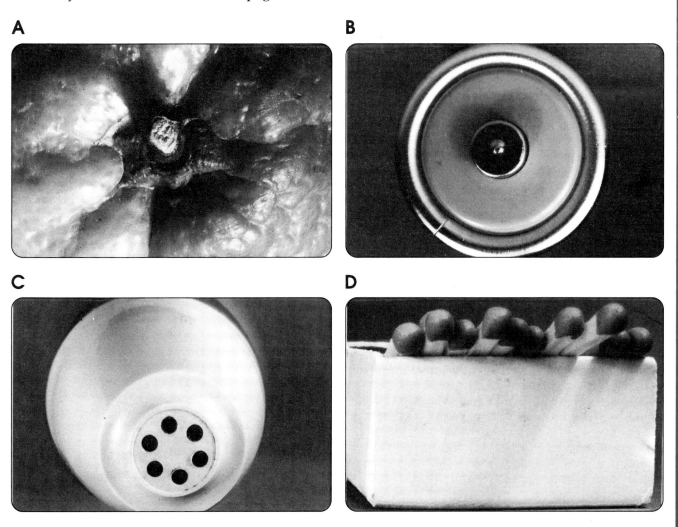

"I found myself looking down on a large object shaped like a small hill. It was made of a shiny metal and had right in the centre, at its highest point, a hole. When I placed a hand inside the hole I found a white powdery substance on the edge."

3 Describe each of the above objects as if you were tiny and did not know what each one was. One has been written for you as an example. Try to write three sentences about each one.

4 Now try to describe the following items in the same way: a calculator, a lipstick, a fork. Describe an object of your own and see if the class can guess what it is.

"*Gulliver's Travels*" was written nearly three hundred years ago. It is now thought of as a children's story, but it was originally written for adults. On his first voyage to Lilliput, Gulliver finds a world of tiny people who turn out his pockets. This passage is difficult in places because it was written so long ago, but can you tell what is going on?

In the right coat pocket of the Great Man-Mountain after the *strictest* search, we found only one piece of coarse cloth, large enough to be foot-cloth for your Majesty's room of state. In the left pocket, we saw a huge silver chest, with a cover of the same metal, which we were not able to lift. We desired it should be opened, and one of us stepping into it, found himself up to *midleg* in a sort of dust which flying up to our faces, set us both a sneezing. In his right waistcoat-pocket, we found a *prodigious* bundle of white thin substances, folded one over another, about the *bigness* of three men, tied with a strong cable, and marked with black figures; which we humbly *conceive* to be writings, every letter almost half as large as the palm of our hands. There were also several round, flat pieces of metal of different *bulk*; some of silver, so large and heavy that we could hardly lift them.

1 In pairs discuss the items found in Gulliver's pockets. Draw labelled diagrams of each item and say what you think each one is.

2 This paragraph was written three hundred years ago and some of the words and phrases which are used in the passage would not be used by us in quite the same way today. With a partner, make a list of the words which are in italics and try to say what we would be more likely to use today.

3 Write your own imaginative story describing your adventures after mysteriously shrinking to a very tiny size.

Since 1917 some photographs taken by two children in Cottingley, Yorkshire, had been believed by many to show real fairies. The photographs were revealed in 1982 to be clever fakes. The two girls continued to argue that they used the photographs to illustrate what they actually saw.

4 Imagine that it is 1982 and the photographs have been proved to be fakes. Write the newspaper headline and article which might have been written after that discovery. Do you have any ideas as to how the photograph might have been faked? If so, you could include the ideas in the article.

5 Many stories exist about tiny fantasy creatures. Try describing a fantasy of your own. You might be able to find some poems or stories from the library to give you ideas.

Of course, shrinking to a tiny size is fine for an adventure story, but it is hardly likely to happen. However, we do talk at times about "feeling small" in front of everyone else. You might have heard people use expressions like, "He made me look small in front of her", or "I felt ten feet tall".

There are a number of occasions when you might "feel small" although you are actually the same size.

For example:
- starting at your new secondary school
- being embarrassed in front of your friends
- being ignored by adults
- being talked about by relatives as if you were not there
- finding it difficult to convince adults you are telling the truth
- being in an awkward situation

6 Write about an occasion when you were made to "feel small". It can be based on an actual memory or you can make it up if you wish.

Now try . . . . . .

7 In pairs role play one or more of the following situations:

(a) The son or daughter is on the phone to a relative thanking them for the birthday present they sent and mother or father is in the background constantly telling them what to say. The relative does not need to be part of the role play.

(b) A pupil has a genuine reason for being late for school (you can decide what it is) but the teacher will not believe the excuse.

(c) A parent and relative are talking about the son or daughter who is sitting in the same room. (For the sake of the role play you can just imagine the son or daughter is there.)

When we say that someone is small and we actually mean he is reduced in size physically we are using language in the LITERAL sense. We mean exactly what we say.

When we say that we "felt small" and we do not mean that we actually became small but that we felt insignificant or humiliated, then we are using language in the FIGURATIVE sense. We do not mean it exactly, but we are giving an impression of what we mean.

In ''The Return of the Antelope'' by Willis Hall, the author describes how three Lilliputians make a voyage from Lilliput to England using Gulliver's charts which he had supposedly left two hundred years earlier. Their boat was destroyed and two children, Philippa and Gerald, take care of them. In the following extract they are looking at a model boat in a window which would be ideal for the journey home of their three guests.

The children pressed their noses against the window and gazed, long and hard, at the vessel on display. The little people did the same.

Inside the office, which was separated from the window by a red-velvet curtain, the assistant manager, Algernon Grimthorpe, was dictating a letter to his lady typist, Mrs Tweedle.

''.... In conclusion, sir, it has always been this company's policy to recommend to its clients the romance of the sailing-ship in preference to the current ill-advised cult for steamship travel,'' said Mr Grimthorpe. ''In short, to see a full rigged schooner, its sails full of wind - ''

Mr Grimthorpe broke off from his dictation to glance over the velvet curtain, fondly, at his pride and joy, the model clipper in the window.

Algernon Grimthorpe smiled proudly.

His smile faded as he caught sight of the two children with their faces pressed against the glass, breathing their hot breath on his window! Happily, he was too annoyed at what he saw to glance further down where three smaller faces also breathed against the glass.

''Shoo!'' mouthed the assistant manager at the children, and: ''Go away at once!'' he added.

Algernon Grimthorpe who, it should be said, was full of his own importance, turned back into the room.

''Where was I, Miss Tweedle?'' he asked.

''Full of wind'', Mr Grimthorpe,'' replied Miss Tweedle.

The assistant manager frowned again and shot a suspicious glance at Miss Tweedle. But the lady typist looked back at him, innocently.

''Harramph!'' went Mr Grimthorpe, clearing his throat disapprovingly, but he decided to drop the matter and continue with his dictation.

''... a full-rigged schooner, its sails full of wind, is a far finer sight than that of a blackened steamship emitting clouds of smoke and propelled through the ocean, or so its devotees would have us believe, powered by nothing but hot air -''

Mr Grimthorpe broke off again as he glanced over the velvet curtain for a second time.

''Well I never!'' he murmured to himself. Those dreadful children had not budged an inch and were still outside, breathing on his window.

''Clear off!'' he mouthed at them, waving his hand angrily to speed them on their way. This time, thank goodness, it did seem as if they were moving on.

''And about time too!'' said Mr Grimthorpe to himself and, turning back to his typist, he said aloud: ''What was I saying, Miss Tweedle?''

''Nothing but hot air, Mr Grimthorpe,'' replied the lady.

This time, the assistant manager thought he did detect a trace of a smile on the typist's face. Before he could pursue the matter though, the bell rang above the door as it was pushed open from outside.

''My goodness gracious!'' murmured Algernon Grimthorpe to himself, as Gerald and Philippa walked in. ''It's those dreadful urchins who were dirtying my window with their breathing!'' And he settled himself at his desk, not wishing to have anything to do with the children.

Miss Tweedle, however, was much more obliging. "Good afternoon," she said with a bright smile as Philippa approached the counter. "And what can I do for you today?"

"We were wondering about the ship you've got in the window?" said Philippa, casting a backward glance at Gerald who had moved towards the velvet curtain.

"The Crimea?" said the typist. "She's an Atlantic schooner. What was it you wished to know about her?"

"We...we were wondering how much it would cost?" replied Philippa hesitantly.

"Well now, that would all depend, wouldn't it," began Miss Tweedle, helpfully, "upon the time of year, for one thing - and there are different classes ..." While she was speaking, the typist had taken out a thick timetable and was now thumbing through the many pages.

With Miss Tweedle thus engaged, and while the unfriendly assistant manager was busy at his desk, Philippa sneaked another glance at her brother. It was Gerald who had successfully smuggled all three of the little people into the shipping office in his pocket. He was now lifting up the bottom of the velvet curtain and, one by one, slipped the three Lilliputians underneath it into the window.

Once inside the window, Spelbush, Brelca and Fistram clambered up on to the deck of the Crimea. They wanted to make sure that the ship would fulfil their requirements: that it could be trusted to carry them across all the oceans between England and their homeland.

While Spelbush tested the sails and rigging and Fistram tried the ship's wheel, Brelca went below and inspected the cabin accommodation.

Inside the office, unaware of all this activity, Miss Tweedle looked up from her timetable and smiled at Philippa. "The summer crossings are the most expensive," she said. "Especially if you wish to travel POSH."

"Posh!" echoed Philippa, puzzled.

"P O S H. That means a cabin on the port side going out, and a cabin on the starboard side coming home," explained Miss Tweedle. "It's the way that all the grand people travel. But, of course, it is very expensive -"

"I'll deal with this, Miss Tweedle," said Mr Grimthorpe getting up from his desk. He stuck his thumbs into his waistcoat pocket importantly, and frowned.

"You're the pair of young hooligans who were finger-marking my window pane and breathing all

over it a moment ago, aren't you?"

Philippa looked at her brother for support.

"No sir," said Gerald, shaking his head firmly. "We were only looking into it."

"And what are you doing now - standing over by that curtain?" added Mr Grimthorpe, suspiciously.

"No reason sir!"

"Come here boy!"

Gerald attempted to signal over the curtain at the little people but Mr Grimthorpe beckoned him with his fore-finger. "At once!"

Gerald walked across, nervously, to join his sister at the counter.

Inside the window, Spelbush, Brelca and Fistram held their breaths and froze like statues as an old couple paused in the street to gaze at the window. The ruse was successful. The man and woman mistook the Lilliputians for model figures that were part of the Crimea's fittings. As the old couple moved on, the little people breathed again and continued their inspection of the ship.

"It's just the vessel to suit our needs!" cried Spelbush, testing the ship's wheel and discovering, to his delight, that it moved easily to his touch.

"There are lots of cabins!" called out Brelca from below.

"There's sufficient hanging space for as big a wardrobe as we wish to take!"

"And the hold's enormous," announced a joyful Fistram as he clambered up on to the deck through a hatchway. "We could store sufficient provisions to take us twice around the world."

The Antelope.

The three little mariners exchanged satisfied smiles at the prospect of putting out to sea again.

But inside the shipping office, things were not going so well.

"And might one enquire," began Mr Grimthorpe, looming over the children, "how you intend to finance this unlikely venture?"

"With our pocket money," said Gerald.

"Pah!"

"And by emptying our money boxes," said Philippa.

"Pocket-money!" sneered the assistant manager. "Money-boxes! Fiddlesticks! Is this some sort of prank? Are you deliberately attempting to waste my time?"

"No sir." The children spoke together.

"Then have you any conception, either of you, how much it would cost - even if you travelled steerage - for two berths on the Crimea sailing from Liverpool to New York?"

Gerald and Philippa looked puzzled.

"We don't want to go anywhere," said Gerald.

"It isn't for ourselves," added Philippa.

"We wondered," continued Gerald, "how much it would be to buy her."

"Buy her!" thundered Mr Grimthorpe. "Buy the Crimea!"

"Not the real one," explained Philippa. "The big toy boat in the window."

"B-b-big toy b-b-boat!" stammered Mr Grimthorpe.

"That ship is not for sale, miss. Neither is it a toy. The vessel in the window is an accurate scale model - correct in every particular detail - of the proudest ship in our passenger fleet. Big toy boat indeed! Miss Tweedle."

"Yes, Mr Grimthorpe?" said the typist nervously, getting to her feet.

"Escort these ignoramuses out of the office!" he bellowed.

1. The children smuggle the Lilliputians into the office in their coat pocket. Can you think of any other way they could have smuggled them into the shop?

2. Try to think of three ways of continuing this story so that the children and the Lilliputians succeed in acquiring the ship. (They actually do in the novel!)

3. This story is set in Victorian times. How many clues can you spot which tell you that this?

4. Find three different sentences spoken by Mr. Grimthorpe which are meant to make the children feel rather small and insignificant.

5. In the story the children have not told any adults about the Lilliputians. Why do you think this is the case?

6. Which of the following descriptive words apply to (a) Miss Tweedle? (b) Mr Grimthorpe? Playful; suspicious; vain; proud; dull; teasing; welcoming; unfriendly; subservient; helpful; pompous; thoughtful; self-satisfied; boring; bitter; amusing; fierce; cunning; careful.

7. In the middle of this extract two old people look in the shop window. Write out the conversation they might have had when they saw the Lilliputians. Attempt this in script form.

A Lilliputian Writes a Poem to Gulliver

See! and believe your Eyes!

See him stride
Vallies wide:
Over Woods,
Over Floods.
When he treads,
Mountains' Heads
Groan and shake;
Armies quake,
Lest his Spurn
Overturn
Man and Steed:
Troops take Heed!
Left and Right
Speed your Flight!
Lest an Host
Beneath his Foot be lost.

Turn'd aside
From his Hide,
Safe from Wound
Darts rebound.
From his Nose
Clouds he blows;
When he speaks,
Thunder breaks!
When he eats,
Famine threats;
When he drinks,
Neptune shrinks!
Nigh thy Ear,
In Mid Air,
On thy Hand
Let me stand,
So shall I,
Lofty Poet! touch the Sky.

Alexander Pope

This poem was written more than 200 years ago. How can you tell? What is a syllable? All words are made up of syllables - they are parts of words which have their own vowel sound. For example: SYL/LA/BLE has three. How many are in your name?
You can count up how many syllables are in each line of the poem. The first line and the last line in each verse all have six syllables. All the other lines have three syllables only.

8 Now write your poem in the same style. Yours should be the other way round - BY Gulliver ABOUT a Lilliputian. Decide whether it is about a man or a woman or a boy or a girl. Then begin as follows:-

GULLIVER WRITES A POEM TO
A LILLIPUTIAN

See! and believe your Eyes!

See him/her stand
On my hand.

This unit is about stories and myths. You will be writing and illustrating your own stories and myths and you will concentrate on full stops, sentences and paragraphs.

Everyone has their own personal story to tell. The following questions are intended to help you remember some of your own.

Have you ever had an accident? Can you remember your first day at school? Have you ever moved house? Have you ever had a pet which died? Have you ever had something embarrassing happen to you? Have you ever been really frightened? Have you ever done anything about which you feel really guilty? Have your parents told you any stories about yourself as a baby?

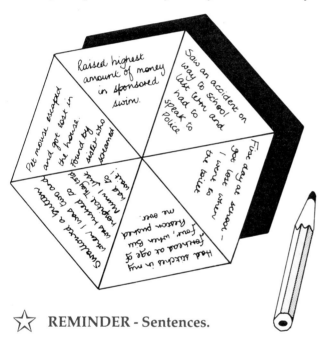

1. Try to remember six "stories" from your life so far. If you like, write them out in the sections of a circle as in the example.

2. In groups of six, if possible, you should each choose a story to tell the others in the group.
☆ You could choose which story to tell by cutting out the story circle, placing a drawing pin in the middle and spinning the circle. You could decide who is to tell the story by placing the six names in a circle and spinning that also.

☆ **REMINDER - Sentences.**

When you are preparing your reading of a story you will have found that you have to be guided by full stops in order to know where to pause and take a breath. There is nothing worse than someone reading a story and pausing in the wrong place. Read your story to a partner again, this time deliberately breathing in the wrong place and you will see the problem. You will know that when you write a story it is also important that you use full stops in the right place. Most people know that *a collection of words which makes complete sense is a sentence,* but it is surprising how many people forget to use sentences when they are writing. The key is to read carefully what you have written, to check your use of full stops.

The following passage is confusing because the full stops have been left out. Read it out loud and try to work out where the pauses should come.

The bee is a symbol of work it is also linked with ideas about death there is a Breton story about bees it tells how bees sprang from the tears shed by Jesus people say you should always tell bees if there is a death in the family they might desert the hive if they are not told

Since time began, people in different countries have been telling stories. Sometimes the stories are told as if they happened to a friend of a friend. Somehow you never seem to be the person to whom something has happened! Similar stories circulate widely. Read these versions of recent stories.

A man and his wife were travelling back from a caravan holiday late at night. They were towing their caravan behind them. Because it was late the wife had gone to bed in the caravan, leaving her husband driving the car on his own.

Sometime after midnight the man stopped for petrol. While he was paying, his wife woke up, looked out of the window and saw an illuminated "Toilet" sign. She pulled a coat around her and, still in her nightdress, ran across the tarmac to the toilet.

Within a few seconds the man returned to the car and, without checking the caravan, drove off into the night.

A young woman was driving home in the rain when she saw an old woman struggling with a basket by the side of the road. She stopped the car and offered to give the old woman a lift.

As they drove along, the driver noticed that the old woman had a gruff voice and was then surprised when the old woman asked if she could smoke in the car. As the cigarette was lit she noticed hairy hands! This was a man dressed as an old woman!

The young woman pretended that she had not noticed, but told the man that she thought one of her back lights was faulty and asked him to check.

When the man reached the back of the car she sped off into the night as fast as she could. She realised that the basket was still in the back seat so she made her way to the nearest police station.

Now try . . . . . .

3 These stories are much better spoken aloud than read. They also need more detail to make them more interesting and could be longer. The caravan story could continue as a zany chase into the night. The other story could continue with a description of what the police found in the basket. In pairs choose one of these stories each and tell a much fuller, more detailed version to each other. For example, when telling the car story think about how you could really build up the tension when the old woman is recognised as a man.

4 Ask any parents, relatives or older friends to tell you any stories they can remember. It would be a good idea to tape the stories, otherwise jot down notes so that you can remember them. You will find that with a little prompting adults have many stories to tell.

5 Make a collection of stories of a similar kind. You could try writing one of your own. Here is an idea for a starting point: For a joke some children move a scarecrow so that it is facing someone's house. It is night time and the scarecrow is facing the house with arms outstretched!

People told stories to each other long before they started to write them down.
Here are three simple stories from different parts of the world.

A story from Pakistan

Once there lived a shopkeeper who used to collect goods from a nearby town. Every day he loaded his goods on to his donkey and brought them home.

One day the donkey slipped and fell in a stream because his load was too heavy. The shopkeeper helped the donkey by carrying some of the goods. This made the load lighter.

"Ah-ha," thought the donkey. "Why don't I pretend to fall every day? This will make my work easier."

So every day the donkey would pretend to trip and fall in the stream and the shopkeeper would always help him.

Soon the shopkeeper realised that the donkey was being crafty. So the next day he loaded the donkey with chapatties. When the donkey sat down in the stream the shopkeeper did not help him.

Now, because chapatties are made from flour they became very heavy in the water. When the donkey tried to stand up, he found he couldn't. The shopkeeper left the donkey in the cold water and ate his lunch, satisfied.

The donkey never tried that trick again.

A story from India

An Indian merchant called Naduk lost a great deal of money through trading. He decided to go abroad to seek better fortune. Before he went he asked his friend, Lakshman, to look after a single bar of silver for him. Even if he made no money abroad, at least that would be waiting for him. When he returned after many months he asked Lakshman for the bar of silver.

"I am so sorry," said Lakshman. "The bar of silver has been eaten by mice."

"That is indeed bad news," said Naduk. "But it is not your fault. Nothing lasts for ever. I must go now to wash the dust of travel off me. Will your son help me to carry my things to the river?"

"Of course," replied Lakshman.

Once Naduk had washed he suggested they rest for a while in the cool of a nearby cave. As soon as the boy entered the cave Nudak pushed him to the ground and closed the entrance with a large rock. He returned to Lakshman.

"Welcome back, Naduk," said Lakshman. "But where is my son?"

"A terrible thing happened," said Naduk. "A hawk swooped down and carried him away. There was nothing I could do."

"You liar," said Lakshman. "How could a hawk carry off a boy?"

Naduk looked straight at Lakshman. "If mice can eat silver then hawks can carry off boys," he said.

A story from Tibet

There was a tortoise that lived in Tibet with his good friends, two birds. One year there was a drought and the two birds prepared to fly off in search of water. They realised the tortoise would have no chance alone, so they thought up a plan. The two birds would each hold one end of a stick and the tortoise would hold on to the middle of it with his mouth. Off they flew, with the tortoise hanging on between them.

They flew over some farms and the farmers looked up.

"Clever tortoise," said the farmers. "See how he lets the birds carry him."

The tortoise felt very proud.

Then they flew over some children.

"Clever birds," said the children. "See how they are carrying the tortoise."

This time the tortoise felt angry. He decided to tell the children it was his idea. He opened his mouth. "Hi ..." was the last word he spoke.

 REMINDER - Paragraphs.

All writing - from infant scribbling to the most complicated novel - builds up from words, to sentences, to paragraphs. As you know, *a collection of words that makes complete sense is a sentence. A group of sentences about the same idea makes up a paragraph.* When you start a new idea in your writing you should start a new paragraph.

You can show that you have started a new paragraph by leaving a line or starting your new paragraph on a new line an inch or so from the margin. Look carefully at when new paragraphs start in the stories printed for you here.

(1) Each of these stories has a simple moral - a point to make about the way people behave. Say what the main point of each story is.

(2) These stories are ideal for young children because they are short and simple. Imagine that you are going to read one of these stories to primary school children. Practise reading it so that you can do so with exactly the right expression to keep their interest. You could practise on a tape-recorder.

(3) There are plenty of stories about animals behaving like humans. Remember Aesop's Fable, "The Hare and The Tortoise"? These stories are often intended to teach a lesson. Try writing one of your own.

Here are some ideas: a vain giraffe keeps looking at its reflection in a lake; a greedy squirrel refuses to share its winter stock of food; a daring chicken does not pay heed to warnings not to walk in the forest.

Remember to produce a rough draft of your writing and check it over carefully.

Now try . . . . . .

4 Make a collection of stories which your class has either found or written for a Story Telling Festival. This could take place in your class or you could visit a primary school to share some of the stories with them.

A Story from Japan.

Hachiko was born in 1923 in Akita in the north of Japan. Akita dogs are famous in Japan. They are fairly large, golden-brown in colour, and they have pointed ears and sharp, clever faces. They are well-known for their loyalty.

It was fortunate for Hachiko when a professor of Tokyo University found him. The professor took him to his house not far from Shibuya station, and there he showed himself a good and kind master. The dog loved him.

Of course Hachiko could not follow his master to the University. But he left the house every morning with the professor and walked along with him as far as Shibuya station. He watched him buy his ticket and disappear towards the train. Then Hachiko used to sit down in the small square and wait for his master's return from work in the late afternoon.

This happened every day. The professor and his dog became a familiar sight, and the story of the faithful animal spread around Shibuya.

Then one afternoon in 1925, there was a tragedy. For some time the professor's health had not been good, and he had a sudden heart-attack at the university. He died before he could be taken home.

Back in Shibuya, the dog waited in front of the station.

Soon the news of the professor's sudden death reached Shibuya. People immediately thought of the poor dog which had followed him every day. Several of them had the same thought. They went to the little square and spoke to the dog - as if he understood them. "Go home, good dog. The professor won't be coming. Go home."

The next morning Hachiko was seen in front of the station, waiting for his master. He waited all day in vain. The following day he was there again. And the next day. And the next. The days became weeks, the weeks months, the months years. Still the dog arrived in front of the station every morning. Still he waited the whole day long, searching among the strange faces for the one that he loved. In rain and sunshine, wind and snow, the faithful animal was there. He was a young dog, ten months old, when his master died; he grew old; but the daily waiting continued.

The dog's faithfulness had an extraordinary effect on the Japanese of Shibuya. He became a public hero - the best-loved figure in the area. Travellers returning to Shibuya after a long absence always asked about him.

"Will Hachiko be there?" they asked, as the train drew in to Shibuya station.

In 1934 the good people of Shibuya asked Teru Ando, a famous Japanese sculptor, to make a statue of their friend Hachiko. He did it gladly, and the statue was set up in front of the station.

For another year Hachiko came every morning to wait, in the shadow of his own statue, for his master. In 1935 the faithful dog died, but not before Ando's work had become famous all over Tokyo.

During the war the statue was melted down, and Ando, the fine sculptor, was killed. But the people of Shibuya remembered Hachiko. They formed a Society for the Replacement of Hachiko's Statue, and the society asked Teru Ando's son, Takeshi Ando, to make the new statue.

Today the fine statue of Hachiko stands in the middle of the busy and friendly square in front of Shibuya station. There are fountains round it, and busy newspaper stands, and usually laughing people, and you will always see somebody telling the story of Hachiko to a child or a grown-up friend. As you look at the statue and read the words below it, you feel that you know a little more about Akita dogs, loyalty, and the people of Japan.

(1) Imagine that the day the second statue was completed there was a news broadcast on the television of just seventy words and a short interview to cover the story. You are the reporter - write out your script.

(2) This story would lose a great deal if it were written in a very shortened form, e.g. "Hachiko was a dog owned by a professor. When the professor died, the dog continued to wait for him at the railway station. The people decided they would build a statue of Hachiko in front of the station." Pick six details from the story which are missing from this version and say why you think they are important to the story.

(3) Similar stories about faithful dogs are told all over the world.
They are often true or based on truth.
For example there is the famous Greyfriars Bobbie of Edinburgh.
Do you have any stories of your own about faithful pets?
Do you have a pet you would describe as faithful?

Some stories are described as "myths" - vivid stories which people told, in order to explain things they saw happening in the world around them. Myths that give an explanation of how the world was made are common in all languages.

Here is a myth from China about how the world was made.

At the beginning of the universe nothing existed but an egg. In the egg was chaos: fire, water, heat, frost and all the other things the world is made of, all mixed up together.

One day the egg hatched, and out of the shell came a giant called Phan Ku, and out spilled all the mixed up things that had been in the egg with him. The light elements sank and formed the earth.

Each day the giant grew ten feet and pushed the sky and the earth further apart, ten feet a day for eighteen thousand years.

When Phan Ku's life came to an end, the various parts of his body became different parts of the universe. From his body came the earth. His head formed the mountains; his breath, the winds; his voice, the thunder; his bones, the rocks; his teeth, the precious stones; his blood, the seas and the rivers; his hair, the trees; his sweat, the rain; his right eye became the moon and his left eye became the sun; his eyebrows became the trees and the plants.

But what about men and women?

When the giant died all the hundreds of tiny fleas living on his body hopped off and became people.

Notice three points about these stories:

✓ 1 They are told very simply.

✓ 2 They use simple language in short paragraphs.

✓ 3 There are no unnecessary words.

Here is another creation myth told by the Indians of Omaha in North America.

In the beginning all men were spirits and the Great Spirit was Wakonda. The spirits moved between heaven and earth looking for somewhere to live in bodily form.

They tried to live on the sun, but they found it was not possible. They tried to live on the moon, but that too was not possible. They descended to the earth but found that there was no land, for it was covered in water. They appealed to Wakonda to help them.

Suddenly a huge rock rose from the water. It burst into flames and the water boiled and became steam. It floated into the air and became clouds. Dry land appeared where grasses and trees began to grow.

The spirits stayed on earth and lived as men and women. They were grateful to Wakonda, the maker of all things.

The next myth is about Arachne from ancient Greece.

Arachne was a very beautiful Greek girl. She was also an expert weaver. One day she was admiring a particularly fine cloth she had woven. ''I am the best weaver in the world,'' she said to herself, quietly.

But Athene, the goddess of crafts, heard her and became very angry. So she disguised herself as an old woman and went to visit Arachne.

''Hello little girl,'' she said. ''What are you doing?''

''I am weaving,'' replied Arachne. ''Is not this the most beautiful cloth you have ever seen?''

''It is beautiful,'' said the old woman. ''But remember that the goddess Athene can weave the finest cloth.''

Arachne said simply, ''I can weave more beautiful cloth than Athene.''

At this Athene became furious. She revealed who she really was and challenged Arachne to a weaving contest.

Athene wove the first piece of cloth; it was very fine indeed. Arachne then wove a piece of cloth; it was finer in every way than that of Athene. Athene saw that she had lost and tore Arachne's cloth into pieces, casting a spell on Arachne. ''You shall shrink until you are a small insect and weave and weave and never finish. You shall live alone in cracks and corners and your work will always be torn apart by other insects.''

Poor Arachne grew smaller and smaller until she ended up as a tiny spider. Ever since that day, spiders have worked endlessly, weaving beautiful, but very fragile cobwebs.

1 One story tells how spiders came to be made - or created. Now write your own story based on the four pictures below, telling how pigs came to be created. Tell your story very simply; write a short paragraph based on each picture.

2 Keeping to a simple style and remembering to use paragraphs, invent your own myth to explain one of the following - or something of your own choice:
- How the robin got its red breast.
- How tobacco was first smoked.
- How fire was discovered.

3 In groups of four or five prepare a reading of the myths which you have written. You could have different people reading different paragraphs, or different people reading out any direct speech, or one person could read the myth and others could mime to it.

In this unit you will be exploring what life might be like on a small island, explaining carefully and describing what you see and feel, and checking about nouns, articles and commas.

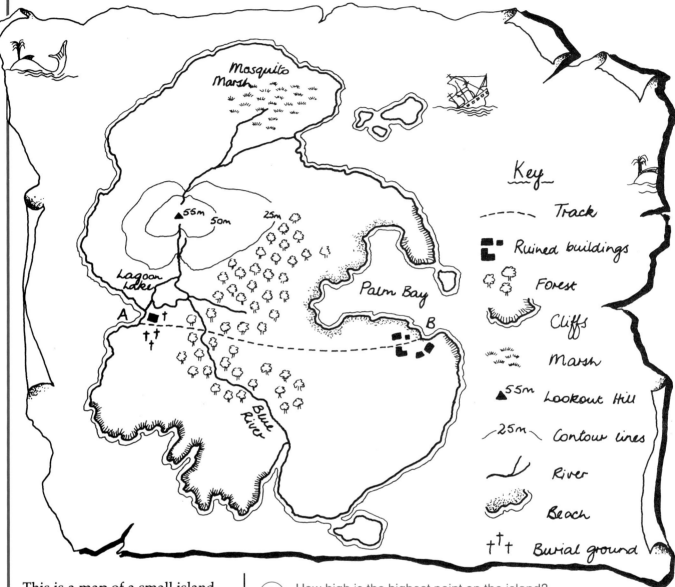

This is a map of a small island. It is just over half a mile across (10 to 15 minutes' walk). The signs or symbols show what is on the island and the key explains what they mean. There is a hill on this island and the two lines show how high it is. These are called **contour** lines.

1. How high is the highest point on the island?

2. Do you think anyone used to live on the island? Explain your reasons.

3. You have just walked from Point A to Point B on this island in an almost straight line. Describe your journey as it really happened. Tell the reader what it felt like and what you saw. Begin "I set off from the beach towards...."

4. You are now going to invent your own island. No one lives on it but people may have lived there once.

☆ Draw a map of an island about the same size as ours. Use our symbols if you wish but invent some of your own as well. Colour your map and include a key to explain every symbol you use.

What?

Where
man has not been
to give
them names
objects
on desert islands
do not
know what they are.
Taking no chances
they stand still
and wait
quietly excited
for hundreds
of
thousands of
years.

Ivor Cutler

Look again at your island. It will probably have many different features and you will know what each one is - a river, a hill, a bay and so on. These naming words are all **COMMON NOUNS**. But explorers give such features their own names as well, for example, Lookout Hill, not just "Hill". These special names are called **PROPER NOUNS** and start with capital letters. There are two other kinds of nouns as well.

The names of emotions you might feel, for example, guilt, loneliness, courage, are nouns but are called **ABSTRACT NOUNS**. There is a fourth category of **COLLECTIVE NOUNS** which are names for groups of things - a **bundle** of sticks, a **shoal** of fish, a **pair** of socks.

Many nouns, but not all, have either the DEFINITE ARTICLE - **the** - or an INDEFINITE ARTICLE - **a** or **an** - in front of them.

☆ REMINDER - Commas.

Using commas is really rather easy. If you need a pause in your writing but the sense of the sentence runs on, you will probably need a comma. You are likely to use commas in three ways.

1. To separate items in a list. Example:
   I collected driftwood, some dry twigs, and a handful of leaves.
2. To separate different parts of a sentence. Example:
   When everything was ready, I lit a fire.
3. To separate words or phrases added to a sentence. Example:
   The fire, to my surprise, flared up immediately.

Make sure you put in all the commas you need, but not more than you need, in your work for this unit.

⑤ You are out on your own in a rowing boat. You see the island and decide to explore it, so you tie up the boat and spend half an hour looking around. When you return to the boat, you find the rope has worked loose and the boat has floated away. You are now stranded. Write an account of your first impressions of the island from when you landed to the moment you realized you had lost your boat.

⑥ Give appropriate names to the features on your island.

⑦ Take one paragraph of your story about arriving at the island and pick out all the nouns.

☆

Alone on your island, you have to make use of anything you can find. You soon become expert at thinking of new uses for ordinary things. Luckily for you, the articles shown in the drawing have all been washed up on your island.

(1) Take each of the above in turn and suggest as many different uses for it as you can. Remember, you are alone on the island.

(2) Write the diary entries for three days of your stay on the island.
On day one you arrive.
On day two something very frightening happens...
On day three you are rescued.

You have now settled on the island. It is not comfortable, but you have built a rough shelter and have enough food and water to last for some time. You hope for rescue, but it could take days or weeks. You decide to keep a diary - or log - of your life on the island. On some days not much happens and the entries are short; then you put in only the things that matter to you such as the weather, any food you find or catch, any unusual happenings and how you feel. On other days you face danger and excitement. You never know what might happen.

Very hot, No wind. Short of water so spent morning searching. Found tiny spring of fresh water. In the afternoon fished, but had no luck. Clouds gathering in the evening so put extra branches on the roof. Went to bed early and slept badly. Storm all night thunder and lightning.

DAY 25. Woken early by cracking noise nearby. Went to see what was happening, but kept out of sight and out of danger. Lucky I did! Terrifying sight on the beach...

SHIPWRECKED
A NEW BOARD GAME

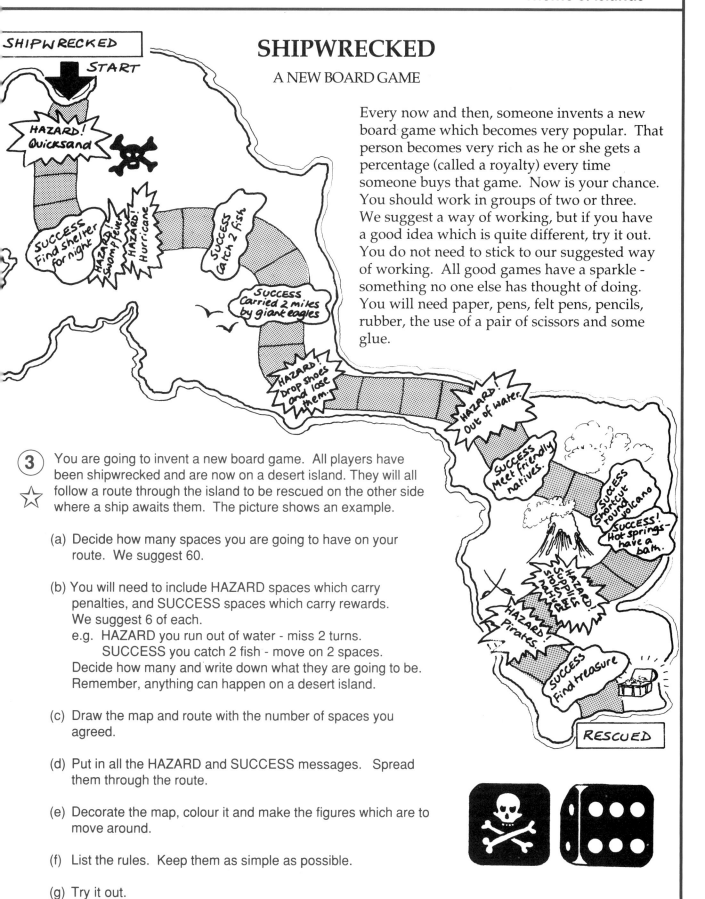

SHIPWRECKED

START

HAZARD! Quicksand

SUCCESS Find shelter for night

HAZARD! Swamp fever

HAZARD! Hurricane

SUCCESS Catch 2 fish

SUCCESS Carried 2 miles by giant eagles

HAZARD! Drop shoes and lose them.

HAZARD! Out of water.

SUCCESS Meet friendly natives.

SUCCESS Shortcut round volcano

SUCCESS! Hot springs - have a bath.

HAZARD! Supplies stolen by apes

HAZARD! Pirates.

SUCCESS Find treasure

RESCUED

Every now and then, someone invents a new board game which becomes very popular. That person becomes very rich as he or she gets a percentage (called a royalty) every time someone buys that game. Now is your chance. You should work in groups of two or three. We suggest a way of working, but if you have a good idea which is quite different, try it out. You do not need to stick to our suggested way of working. All good games have a sparkle - something no one else has thought of doing. You will need paper, pens, felt pens, pencils, rubber, the use of a pair of scissors and some glue.

(3) ☆ You are going to invent a new board game. All players have been shipwrecked and are now on a desert island. They will all follow a route through the island to be rescued on the other side where a ship awaits them. The picture shows an example.

(a) Decide how many spaces you are going to have on your route. We suggest 60.

(b) You will need to include HAZARD spaces which carry penalties, and SUCCESS spaces which carry rewards. We suggest 6 of each.
   e.g. HAZARD you run out of water - miss 2 turns.
         SUCCESS you catch 2 fish - move on 2 spaces.
   Decide how many and write down what they are going to be. Remember, anything can happen on a desert island.

(c) Draw the map and route with the number of spaces you agreed.

(d) Put in all the HAZARD and SUCCESS messages. Spread them through the route.

(e) Decorate the map, colour it and make the figures which are to move around.

(f) List the rules. Keep them as simple as possible.

(g) Try it out.

The following extract is from *'' Swallows and Amazons''* by Arthur Ransome. The book is about the adventures of some children aged between seven and thirteen. Four of them are sailing in a small dinghy called *Swallow* to a deserted island in the lake. There they plan to set up the camp for a few days. In the extract they are sailing around the island looking for a safe place to land.

The island was covered with trees and among them there was one tall pine which stood out high above the oaks, hazels, beeches and rowans. They had often looked at it through the telescope from Darien. The tall pine was near the north end of the island. Below it was a little cliff, dropping to the water. Rocks showed a few yards out from the shore. There was no place to land there.

"Now, Mister Mate," said Captain John, "we must keep a good look-out."

"Sing out like anything if you see any rocks under water, Roger," said the mate.

John steered to pass between the island and the mainland, not too near the island so as not to lose the wind. In a moment or two *Swallow* was slipping through smooth water, though there was still enough wind to keep her slowly moving. A little more than a third of the way along the eastern shore of the island there was a bay, a very small one, with a pebbly beach. Behind it there seemed to be a clearer space among the trees.

"What a place for a camp," said Susan.

"Good landing too," said John, "but no good if the wind came from this side. We'll sail right round the island first to see if there is anything better."

"Rocks ahead," sang out Roger, pointing to some that were just showing above water. John steered a little farther from the shore.

The sides of the island were steep and rocky. That little bay seemed to be the only place where it would be possible to land a boat. There were rocky cliffs, like the Peak in Darien, only much smaller, with heather on them and little struggling trees. At the south end of the island the rocks grew smaller and then suddenly rose again into a promontory of almost bare stone. At this southern end the island seemed to have been broken up into a lot of little islands. John sailed on till he was well beyond the last of them and then began hauling in the sheet, putting the helm down, and bringing *Swallow* round below the island.

"That first place is the only good one on that side," said Susan.

HOW A WRITER WORKS

(1) One of the tricks of telling a good story is to get across essential information while you are telling it. This extract is about looking for a landing place, but we also learn what job each of the three people does in the boat. Test it. List the three people and what their jobs are.

(2) We also find out about safe and dangerous landing places. Look through the passage and list what the writer tells us will make a landing place safe and what will make it dangerous.

(3) The writer means us to guess why John sails *"well beyond"* the last of the small islands before turning. Why does John do this?

(4) This book was written more than fifty years ago. Even in that comparatively short time, language has changed. Pick out any words or expressions which show that it was not written recently.

Now try . . . . . .

5 From the extract it is possible to work out the route of the *Swallow* and some details of the island. Try it. Draw the island including as much detail as you can, show the direction North, and draw a dotted line to represent the route of the *Swallow*.

If you put a shell to your ear, it is said that you can hear the sound of the sea.

The Shell

And then I pressed the shell
Close to my ear
And listened well.
And straightway, like a bell,
Came low and clear
The slow, sad murmur of far distant seas
Whipped by an icy breeze
Upon a shore
Wind-swept and desolate.
It was a sunless strand that never bore
The footprint of man,
Nor felt the weight
Since time began
Of any human quality or stir,
Save what the dreary winds and waves incur.
And in the hush of waters was the sound
Of pebbles rolling round;
For ever rolling with a hollow sound;
And bubbling sea-weeds as the waters go,
Swish to and fro
Their long cold tentacles of slimy grey.
There was no day;
Nor ever came a night
Setting the stars alight
To wonder at the moon;
Was twilight only, and the frightened croon,
Smitten to whimpers, of the dreary wind
And waves that journeyed blind...
And then I loosed my ear - Oh, it was sweet
To hear a cart go jolting down the street.

James Stephens

Now try . . . . . .

(6) Where is James Stephens really, and how do you know?

(7) Do you think he would prefer to be on his imagined sea shore or where he is really? Give your reasons.

(8) The shore where James Stephens finds himself is not a welcoming place. List all the words you can find that show this.

9 Now you try daydreaming about something. Write down your impressions of your daydream. Have you written a poem?

4.1 Wall Magazine.

In this unit you will be working with one or two others writing pieces which will become parts of a Class Wall Magazine. You will need to make sure your work *LOOKS* good on the wall and is carefully checked so there are no mistakes.

You will work through a series of tasks as follows:

- Task 1 Form working groups.
- Task 2 Choose your subjects.
- Task 3 Who does what?
- Task 4 Editing and improving.
- Task 5 Producing final versions.
- Task 6 Putting the wall magazine together.

TASK 1. Form working groups.

Form groups of two or three people. Make sure your group has a clear working space, and you will be able to talk to each other without annoying neighbours.
You will need the following:
sheets of A4 paper; pencils; rubber; pens; felt pens; ruler; use of a pair of scissors and glue; use of a word-processor if possible.

 ## TASK 2. Choose your subjects.

The wall magazine must catch your eye; anyone who sees it must want to look more closely.
It should be varied and attractive.
Your group must now choose to do at least **THREE** different things.

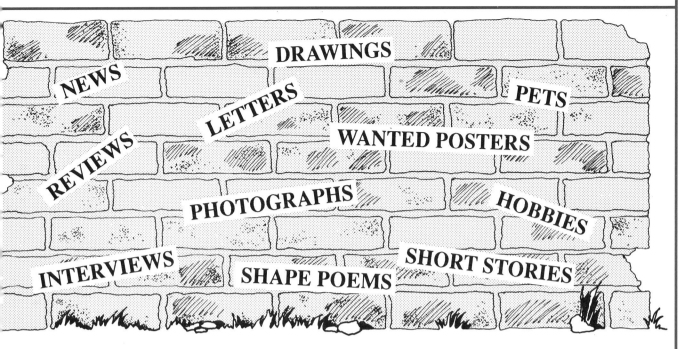

NEWS
DRAWINGS
LETTERS
PETS
REVIEWS
WANTED POSTERS
PHOTOGRAPHS
HOBBIES
INTERVIEWS
SHORT STORIES
SHAPE POEMS

You may have other ideas as well. Share your ideas together before making decisions. **THINK BIG!** Remember that whatever you produce will need to be **SEEN EASILY** when it is on the wall. Think about how it could look when you make your choices. For example, a shape poem will look more eye-catching than just a poem.
Decide on your choices and hand a list of them to your teacher with your names at the top.

TASK 3. Who does what?

Your group needs to share the work out. Decide who does what. Then start. Your first draft will be a rough copy. Do not worry too much about how it looks as long as someone else can read and understand it easily. You may wish to change words or sentences, so cross or rub out if you wish.

This draft needs to show how it will appear for the Wall Magazine, even though it is in rough. Your work needs to make an **IMPACT.**

Wall Magazine.

TASK 4. Editing and Improving.

This is a very important stage.

Draft.

> ## My Londons BURNING!!!!
>
> ① A bewilderd young child
>   her nature mild!
>   Stumbled down "Old London St."
>
> ② The flames were a leaping
>   The smoke was a creaping
>   Along her "Old London St"
>
> ③ The child was weeping
>   NO-ONE was sleeping
>   As burnt down "Old London St"
>
> ④ As away they ran
>   She was the only one
>   Who stayed with "Old London St"
>
> ⑤ The memorys they came
>   again & again
>   Reminders of "Old London St"
> ⑥ They found her that morn
>   cold & forlorn
>   Crying for her "Old London St"

Edited draft.

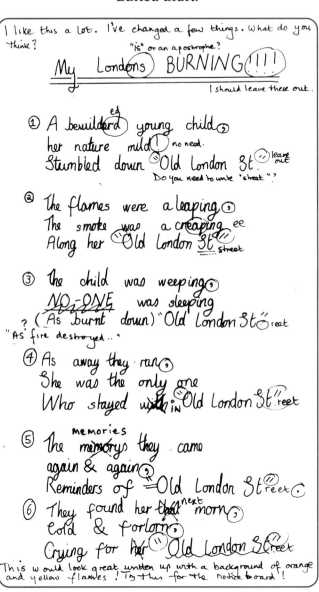

Hand your draft to another member of your group when it is ready. In turn you will get someone else's draft.

This is what you must do with it:

1 In general - do you like it? If you can, write down ways in which it might be improved.
2 Think about the **IMPACT** it will make when part of a wall magazine. Can you suggest ideas about how it might be more eye-catching?
3 Go through the work very carefully and correct any mistakes. If you are not sure of a word, check it in a dictionary.

You have now edited your draft.

TASK 5. Producing final versions.

When you get your edited draft back, look at all the suggestions and corrections carefully. You might want to discuss some of them with your group or your teacher. Can you make it better still in any way?

Remember, you want it to make an **IMPACT.**

Now **CAREFULLY** do your work again as well as you can. When you have finished, it will be ready for display.

TASK 6. Putting the Wall Magazine together.

This will involve everyone working together.
A suggested plan is as follows:

1 Collect all finished work.
2 Divide the work into groups.
3 Decide on overall headings.
4 Agree on a rough overall appearance for the wall magazine.
5 Share tasks among the groups. You will need large headings;
   items of work will need to be arranged in their groups and stuck
   on to large sheets of paper.
6 Put up the completed Wall Magazine.

In this unit you will become a time traveller, able to travel backwards and forwards in time. You will also give some thought to the uses of different tenses in your writing.

Imagine that you are the proud owner of a time machine. Inside the machine there is a dial which allows you to visit any time in the past or future.

First colony on the Moon.

Man travels to other Galaxies.

Britain at war. The Battle of Britain.

1940

The Battle of Hastings.

1066

2001

Life forms found on other planets.

The glories of the Ancient World.

2000BC

The Great Pyramids of Egypt built.

2290

The Era of Robots.

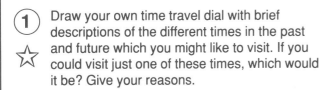

Now try . . . . . .

(1) ☆ Draw your own time travel dial with brief descriptions of the different times in the past and future which you might like to visit. If you could visit just one of these times, which would it be? Give your reasons.

2 ☆ If you travelled into the future, to a time when you are older, would you be able to meet yourself? It sounds far-fetched but anything is possible in your imagination. Write out the conversation you might have with yourself if you went forward in time. The results could be quite funny and confusing.

One of your journeys takes you into the future and you visit a museum. The museum has a special room which shows how people used to live in the 1990s. There are photographs and objects with descriptions to go with them.

THE TWENTIETH CENTURY

In the 1990s humans actually still had hair on their heads. It served very little purpose and was merely decorative. Humans spent much time and energy taking care of their hair and worrying about their hairstyle. Here is a typical hairstyle of the 1990s.

Before the invention of teleportation in 2010, transport was very primitive. Here is a typical means of transport called a car. It was very slow, noisy and dirty.

Notice that the descriptions can tell us something about the future world to which you have travelled.

(3) Choose ten more objects which might have been on display in the museum, all from the 1990s. Draw them or use pictures from magazines then write the descriptions which go with them. Here are some ideas: animals, food, grass, blackboards, cigarettes. Try to write at least three sentences about each one.

(4) When you have finished your list, exchange it with someone else in the class. Your job is now to try and work out as much as you can about the future world your partner has invented. From the descriptions above, for example, we can work out that there is some new means of travelling called teleportation and humans no longer have hair. Write a paragraph about the future world suggested by your partner's list.

5.2 Future and Past.

You have travelled into the future and when you visit the twentieth century museum you hear two people, Alpha and Zeta, having the following conversation as they walk around the museum.

Alpha: Come over here and look around.

Zeta: What is it?

Alpha: I don't know. It is some form of organic matter with paper wrapped around it.

Zeta: Some sort of food?

Alpha: Perhaps it is a type of medicine.

Zeta: Look it up in the guide book.

Alpha: Let me see... Exhibit 304. It says here it is a cigarette, or known in slang as a "cig" or a "fag". People used to put it in their mouths, set fire to it and breathe in the smoke.

Zeta: Ugh! How revolting! What is the point? Was it good for them?

Alpha: No, it says here that it sometimes made them ill and they died.

Zeta: It must have been a strange time to live in. Look over there. I know what that is. It's a gun.

Now try . . . . . .

1 With a partner, continue the conversation as the two people walk around the museum. When you have finished you could read the result to the rest of the class.

2 ☆ Sometimes museums have special exhibitions. Design a poster for the twentieth century museum which advertises a showing of "Life in the 1990s". Examples to mention might be sport, pop music, methods of transport - or perhaps a reconstruction of life in the 1990s.

You have travelled to the future. It is now time to make a brief trip into the past. When you step out of your time machine here is the scene which greets you.

Now try . . . . . .

3 Describe what you think is going on in the picture.

4 Make a list of the things we have in our time which the people in the picture probably did not have in their time, e.g. television.

5 Copy the picture (trace it if you wish). Imagine that you suddenly appear on the scene. Add a drawing of yourself and your time machine to the picture you have drawn.
☆

6 Describe what happened when you arrived on the scene.

7 Draw a labelled diagram of your time machine - both the inside and the outside. It may look very ordinary from the outside but be completely different inside!

In the following passage, the girl Janice is actually a visitor from a future time on earth, but nobody knows this.

Miss Sutherland walked into the room, dumped her books on her desk and looked out over the class of first years. Some were perched on the window sills. Some were standing in a tight group around a girl sitting at a desk, shrieking with nervous laughter at a magazine hidden in the middle of them. Some were running around, playing a game of tag which had started on their first day and was still going two days later.

Nobody wanted to be the one to be tagged before the lesson started.

Everybody was talking, laughing, screaming, giggling and most of them were moving at the same time.

Except one, Miss Sutherland noticed again. One who sat quietly at the back of the class, with her exercise book on the table. She watched the other children in the class and she watched the teacher. There was a little smile on her face.

Miss Sutherland was a geography teacher. Her room was on the second floor, at the top of the building, and the windows all along one side looked over Redbridge Park. It was Miss Sutherland's second year at Redbridge Park Girls' Comprehensive School, and she found that she did not get much chance to look over the park, at the world outside. She looked out instead over her class of first years, who all seemed eager for something, if not for geography. Miss Sutherland swung into her routine.

"ALL RIGHT SIT DOWN ON A CHAIR BY A TABLE NOT THE WINDOWSILLS STOP THAT GIVE ME THAT COME ON TEN MINUTES OF THE LESSON GONE ALREADY WHY DO I ALWAYS HAVE TO SHOUT BEFORE YOU DO ANYTHING COME ON!"

That last, extra loud "ON" was the accepted signal. Everything settled down. Miss Sutherland began the lesson.

"You are just beginning at this school. It always seems to me a good idea to begin in the first year with the very beginnings of geography: in the first years of time itself on Earth, when the Earth began." Miss Sutherland began to get into her stride. She was a good teacher, and she knew she was on to a winner with the prehistoric stuff. Children of all ages are fascinated by ideas of what the world was when they were not on it.

"I want you to have some idea - just a little idea of how long ago it was when the earth began. So I now want you to tell me how many years you think a million days make."

Miss Sutherland pointed to one girl after another to have a guess. She wanted them to see how easy it was to talk about a million without realising how many a million was.

Back came the answers thick and fast.

"Twenty years."

"Eight years."

"Fifty years."

"Two hundred years."

"Any advance on two hundred years?" said Miss Sutherland with a smile. As usual, nobody had any notion of how long it was.

"One more guess," she said, as she noticed that the quiet girl at the back had her hand up.

"Good," thought Miss Sutherland. "She's going to join in. I hope the others don't laugh at her and put her off trying again."

"What is your guess Janice?" she said. As she had feared, the class fell quite silent, and swung around to look at the girl, who sat quietly smiling at the back of the class. Nobody really knew quite what to make of her yet, and so everybody wanted to hear what she had to say.

"It isn't a guess, Miss," she said. "It is 2,737 years 311 days."

Miss Sutherland's jaw dropped. The class gasped. Nobody giggled or jeered. They swung back towards the teacher to see what her reaction was.

"Well, I'll have to take your word for it, Janice," she said. "I've never worked it out. I was going to say 'over 2,500 years'. How on earth do you know exactly?"

Janice smiled vaguely.

"I suppose I must have read it somewhere," she said. The rest of the class burst into applause. It wasn't often that anybody in a class could surprise a teacher with what she knew. She was their classmate, and even if she was a bit different they could share in her knowledge, and be reflected in her little bit of glory.

In that moment the class adopted her. She became truly one of them. Miss Sutherland saw this happen and was glad that it had. Because of her gladness she did not think any more about Janice's answer. Not at the time anyway. Not until she had other reasons for remembering.

She went on with the lesson and the class listened with real attention.

"Two and a half thousand years ago was over five hundred years before Jesus was born. The few people who lived in England then still lived in huts of mud and stones. And that is only a million days. To have some idea of how long a million years is you will have to imagine a time 365 times longer than that."

"And you'll have to add 684 days for the leap years," said Janice quietly; so quietly that nobody noticed.

"The earth is about five thousand million years old," said Miss Sutherland, "so if you were able to imagine 365 times 2,500 years you will have to be able to imagine a time five thousand times longer than that to get a real idea of the time it has taken the world to get this far."

Nobody could imagine of course. Well, almost nobody.

"Miss," said a small girl at the front of the class, "can I do a project on dinosaurs?"

"I'll do it with you Mary," shouted about six others at once.

"Well, I'm glad you're all interested in life on earth before human beings," said Miss Sutherland. "But don't forget that a lot happened besides dinosaurs. Dinosaurs roamed the Earth for 135 million years. So far people have managed about two million. But a lot happened before the dinosaurs, and a lot happened after them."

Miss Sutherland began giving out copies from the pile of books she had brought in at the beginning of the lesson.

"I'm afraid some of you are going to have to share for a little while," she said as she gave the last one out. "Last year's first years lost so many of these we had to order a lot more. They should be in soon, but they haven't come yet so we'll have to manage without."

Groans of disappointment came from the children who weren't lucky enough to get a copy. The pips went for the end of the lesson and the children piled out of the classrooms. It was breaktime. One or two stayed to talk.

"Miss, did you see any of the Dr. Who adventures on the telly? This man brought dinosaurs back through time and made them appear in London. The models were really good."

Miss Sutherland picked up a few pieces of paper off the floor and got ready to go down to the staffroom for a welcome cup of tea.

"Yes, a good model is as close as anybody will ever get to seeing a dinosaur in the flesh," she said. "As far as the experts can tell dinosaurs were extinct on this earth 130 odd million years before people put in an appearance. Nobody has ever seen a living dinosaur."

"Bye Miss," called the last children as they disappeared down the stairs. Miss Sutherland yawned, locked her classroom door and turned to follow them. Janice was standing quietly beside her. Miss Sutherland flinched in surprise.

"Oh Janice, you gave me a fright. I thought everybody had gone."

"To see a real dinosaur, Miss," she said, "that would be something, wouldn't it?"

"It certainly would Janice."

"Bye Miss."

Janice paused at the top of the stairs.

"North Downs School have got six spare copies of that book you gave out, Miss. Yours will be here next week, so why not borrow theirs until then? Bye."

Miss Sutherland was very thoughtful as she walked slowly down the stairs towards the staffroom.

"Janice Jennings," she said quietly to herself, "there is something very unusual about you."

She rang North Downs School at lunchtime. The school secretary put her through to the Head of Geography who was very helpful.

"Yes, as luck would have it we have got some spare copies. I know we have because I gave that book out myself this morning to a first year class."

"What are your first years like this year?"

"Oh worse than usual - as usual! But at least one thing happened this morning that has never happened before. I was doing the bit about how many years a million days were, you know, and this child at the back suddenly piped up with '2737 years 311 days not forgetting 684 days for the leap years'!"

Miss Sutherland shivered suddenly. She replied quietly:

"The child was right. I have just worked it out. It took me over half an hour. Can you tell me what the child's name is?"

"Yes, Joan Jeffryes. Of course I don't know all their names yet but there is something rather unusual about her."

Miss Sutherland was thinking. It wasn't the same name so they weren't closely related. Unless... Oh no, she was letting her imagination run away with her. She had just two more questions to ask the teacher at the other school.

"Can you tell me what time you gave out the books this morning?"

"Yes certainly. It was half an hour ago, the last period of the morning."

The tip of an ice cold finger seemed lightly to touch the nape of her neck.

"And how many copies can you let me have?"

The answer came back swiftly, cheerfully, without hesitation.

"Six."

① Notice at the start of the story how the scene is set in the classroom. Write down three sentences of your own each starting with "Some..." which describe the scene at the start of the lesson in your classroom.

② Janice only speaks a few times in the story. Copy down what she says each time. Remember that the words she speaks are in speech marks.
What rules do we need to follow when we are punctuating speech?

③ From what she says and from the way she behaves, what clues are there in the passage that Janice is not an ordinary girl?

④ Write down three facts we learn about Miss Sutherland. Is she a good teacher in your opinion?

⑤ Imagine that you were one of the pupils in the class. Write the entry which you made in your diary when you went home that evening.

⑥ How do you think the story will continue?
You might like to compare your version with the actual story called "Time Out" by Robin Chambers.

REMINDER - Tenses.

When we write or talk about the past we use the past tense.
e.g. Yesterday I broke a chair leg.

When we write or talk about the present we use the present tense.
e.g. Today my father is buying some strong glue.

When we write about what is going to happen we use the future tense.
e.g. Tomorrow I shall mend it.

It is useful to know about tenses when you are writing because it is usually not a good idea to mix up tenses when you are telling a story, unless you do so on purpose.

In the following passage there is one verb which sounds out of place. Can you tell which one it is? Why is it out of place?

The machine came to a stop at last. I undid my safety harness, opened the door and went out. I was surprised to find myself in a field of corn, with an old farmhouse in the distance. I walk to a path at the edge of the field and made my way towards the house.

(7) Look back at the excerpt from the short story you have just read. Try to find an example of each tense. Copy out the sentence and underline the verb saying which tense is being used.

(8) Look back at the writing you have done so far in this unit. Try to find out examples of the different tenses. Is there any tense you have not used yet?

(9) You are now sitting at your time machine controls. It is up to you where you travel. Tell the story of your adventure when you travelled in time. Use some of the ideas we have already discussed in the unit, but you should think up your own ideas as well.

In this unit you will enter the world of spies and codes. You will also gain some practice in giving information clearly and accurately, and find out about body language.

```
THESE CRETFI LEWILL BELE FTBE HINDT HEBEN CHIN THEP ARK
```

You have followed a spy into a park and you have seen him or her place the above message for a contact under a stone. You try to read the message but it is in code.
Can you crack the code? Try reading it aloud.

Here is the same message in a different code.
This one is harder.

To decipher the code you need to draw patterns and then insert the letters of the alphabet.

(You can find the answers on page 96.)

Now try . . . . . .

 (1) Write out a message of at least fifteen words using the pattern code and give it to someone else in the class to translate.

(2) Invent your own code. Write a message using your own code and give it to someone in the class to see if they can translate it.

3 This activity is called "Alibi". You need to decide on a particular incident - for example, the classroom was broken into last night and some furniture was damaged. Two members of the class are then sent out of the room. They decide on their joint alibi, while the rest of the class decide on how to question them. They are then brought back into the classroom one at a time for questioning. They are NOT allowed to communicate until the court has come to a verdict. Are they guilty or not guilty? In other words, can the class manage to break down their alibi?

My neighbour Mr. Normanton

My neighbour Mr. Normanton
Who lives at ninety five
'S as typical an Englishman
As any one alive.

He wears pin stripes and a bowler hat,
His accent is sublime,
He keeps a British bulldog
And British Summer Time.

His shoes are always glassy black
(He never wears the brown);
His brolly's rolled slim as a stick
When he goes up to town.

He much prefers a game of darts
To mah jongh or to chess.
He fancies Chelsea for the cup
And dotes on G and S.

Roast beef and Yorkshire pudding are
What he most likes to eat.
His drinks are tea and British beer
And sometimes whisky (neat).

Out of a British briar-pipe
He puffs an Empire smoke,
While gazing at his roses (red)
Beneath a British oak.

And in his British garden,
Upon St George's Day,
He hoists a British Union Jack
And shouts ''Hip, hip hooray''.

But tell me, Mr. Normanton
That evening after dark,
Who were those foreign gentlemen
You met in Churchill Park?

You spoke a funny language
I could not understand;
And wasn't that some microfilm
You'd hidden in your hand?

And then that note I saw you pass
Inside a hollow tree!
When I jumped out, you turned about
As quick as quick could be.

Why did you use a hearing-aid
While strolling in the park
And talking to that worried-looking
Admiralty clerk?

The day you took the cypher-book
From underneath a stone,
I'm certain, Mr. Normanton
You thought you were alone.

Your powerful transmitter!
The stations that you call!
I love to watch you through the crack
That's in my bedroom wall.

Oh, thank you Mr Normanton,
For asking me to tea.
It's really rather riveting
To clever chaps like me.

What? Will I come and work for you?
Now please don't mention pay.
What super luck I left a note
To say I'd run away!

Is that a gun that's in your hand?
And look! A lethal pill!
And that's a real commando-knife?
I say, this is a thrill!

Of course I've never said a word
About the things you do.
Let's keep it all secret
Between just me and.....

Charles Causley

(4) What do you think happens at the end of the poem? Can you tell what Mr Normanton is thinking in the last three verses?

(5) Draw two columns on your page and place the headings "Mr Normanton's Cover" and "The real Mr Normanton" at the top of each. Make notes in your own words to describe what Mr Normanton's "cover" was and in the other column make notes which describe how we know that the real Mr. Normanton was a spy. Be prepared to explain why you have included each detail.

(6) Try writing your own poem about a spy pretending to be something else. Keep to four lines in each verse and try using rhyme in the way Charles Causley does.

Spy Dossier.

NAME .... William Shenton ....

GOES BY THE
NAME OF ...... James thomas ....

MAIN ADDRESS .... 43 Kynastor Road ...
enfield ...

OTHER ADDRESS .... 2 front st ....
Durham ...

EDUCATION ... went to Priory Comp., Northam ...

FAMILY .... none Known ...

KNOWN COVER ... works iregularly as window cleaner ...

COUNTRY OF
ORIGIN ..... british ....

DISGUISES has been Known to pose as traveling Salesman

REASONS FOR
SUSPICION plenty of money to travel a lot. Contacts Known Spies

PHONE TAPPED   YES/~~NO~~ ....

DETAILS OF INTERESTING TELEPHONE
CALLS .... 18-1-90 Call to Amserdam - about money deals.
?

RECOMMENDED ACTION ....

---

(1) The agent who filled in this form did so in a hurry. He made a number of mistakes (use of capital letters, spellings, punctuation, incomplete sentences). Before you place it in a file, your job is to write out a correct copy and state what action you recommend.

(2) Complete your own spy dossier about a character of your choosing. You could use a photograph from a magazine or a newspaper on which to base the character.

(3) Make a file containing different information about your invented spy. Examples of details you could include are a coded message which you managed to copy, a letter from the spy to a friend, finger prints, details of the spy's car, photographs, a diagram of the spy's house showing where you have planted listening devices.

Here is a map showing the route taken by your spy when you followed him or her.

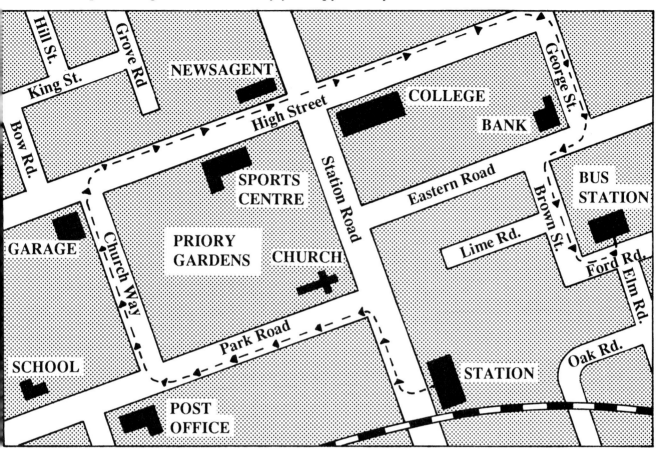

Here is the description which was written by an agent who followed another spy.

I waited outside Boots the Chemist across the road from the station. Suspect X came out of the station, turned left and walked along the High Street heading North. X took the first turning left off the High Street into Brent Street. About one hundred yards along the road he stopped to go into the Post Office. He came out and continued along Brent Street until he came to the first turning on the right. This took him past the park. At the end of the park at the T junction he turned right on to Malin Road. He kept going until he came to the High Street again. By now I thought he might have guessed I was following him because he stopped and looked in the window of Burton's at the corner of Malin Road and the High Street. He passed Brent Street without turning off and stopped again at the newsagents (Martins) just after Brent Street. Suddenly he started walking at a brisker pace, dashed across the road and disappeared into the station. I followed him, but he caught the train to London. It was obvious that he must have known the exact times of the trains.

Now try . . . . . .

(4) You want to get the information on the map to your boss using a code. Write the information out in sentences and then translate it into your chosen code.

5 In pairs or singly, your job is to draw a map of the area showing the route taken by the spy, X. Show the various stops he made. Mark as much as you can on the map. You will need to make rough copies first.

6.3 Messages.

When we speak we also move our hands, change the expressions on our faces and generally move our bodies as we are speaking. These movements are known as "Body Language" or Non Verbal Communications (NVCs). Sometimes they give messages which are more important than the words being spoken. Just think of how difficult it is to tell a lie without giving yourself away.

Another complication is that some gestures have different meanings, depending on which country the person comes from.

A closed hand has no particular meaning in the British Isles, but if you used it in France it would mean that you were afraid; in Greece you would be saying "Good!" ; in Tunisia you would mean "Slowly!" and in Italy you would be asking a question.

You need to be careful about gestures. If you pull at your earlobe in Spain or Greece, you may well be insulting someone!

If you were French this would tell you 'nothing' as it means Zero!

When you visit Japan make sure that you know that this means 'money'!

In the United States of America this would tell you that everything was fine - OK!

① Imagine you are spying on someone who stops to talk to a contact. They are some distance away from you, so you cannot hear what they are saying but you can see their movements. It is not a long conversation. Write a report describing the bodily movements of the two people. When you have read what you have written, is it possible to guess what they were talking about?

② You have to prepare a "Body Language Guide" for some visitors from overseas. Select a list of six common gestures which are important for them to understand, describe them and explain their meanings.

③ Make a collection of signs and gestures from other countries, together with their meanings. There may be people in your class with knowledge of other cultures who can help to start it off.

Passing on secret messages.

Even a coded message may be deciphered. You need to pass messages on secretly so that they do not fall into the wrong hands.

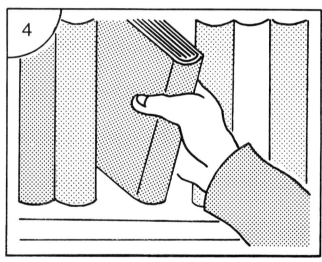

The drawings above show one method of hiding a message, though if you try it please use an old book that nobody wants any more!

(4) Invent your own way of hiding a message which can then be picked up by your contact. Illustrate your method in four simple pictures and then write a sentence or two of explanation underneath each one.

(5) EITHER write a story called "A Spy's Day" OR copy out the following passage and use it for the start of your story. You will need to choose your own title:

Having let the alarm clock ring itself to sleep again, I left home at the last minute as usual, but on that fateful Tuesday I never reached school. Instead I was caught up in a world of fear. It began when I overheard a conversation between two sinister-looking men sitting in front of me on the bus.

This unit is about the times when life seems unfair. You will find emphasis on understanding how people feel, as well as direct speech, letter writing, and skimming for information.

1 Write down what you think each of the people in the pictures is saying.

2 ☆ What do you think the other person in each of the first three pictures is thinking?

3 In each of the pictures we could say that one person is "picking on" someone else because of what has happened to him or her.

4 Draw your own set of pictures showing a similar chain of events, but using different characters. Include speech bubbles to show what the characters are saying.

5 Give the pictures the title "It's Not Fair".

6 The pictures and speech bubbles will give you the outline of a simple story called "It's Not Fair". Write that short story using speech marks instead of speech bubbles and description instead of pictures.

7 Cover the figure on the left in the photograph with your hand or a piece of paper. Imagine that the photographer had only shown the group on the right. In pairs decide what you might have thought was going on without the other figure in the photograph. Notice how the meaning of the photograph is changed when you uncover the figure on the left.

8 Give the photograph a title.

9 Imagine that the boy on the left goes home and makes an entry in his diary about the day. It starts "Why me?" Continue the entry he made.

10 In the end the boy in the photograph writes to an advice column in a magazine. Write the letter and the reply he receives.

Now try . . . . . .

11 Have you ever felt on the outside of a group of friends? If the answer is yes, describe the incident in detail and describe how you felt. If you prefer, write about someone else you have known who has been on the outside of a group. Describe what happened.

The Lock Out.

Colin Thiele

By eleven o'clock that night Jim realised how slowly time went when you were on your own. Boomer called in for a while before tea to make sure Jim would be fit for the big match in the morning, but apart from that he spent the evening alone. He washed the dishes, fed the cat, watched TV, polished his boots, put out the milk bottles, locked the door and sauntered about restlessly from room to room. It was a shock to see how dark and empty the house could be. Then, at the last minute, he remembered that his football shorts hadn't been washed after Thursday's practice, so he hastily doused them in detergent and warm water, rubbed the slide marks and dirty patches from the seat and then drew them out looking over-scrubbed and bleached. After rinsing them and squeezing them as dry as he could, he carried them up to the lounge, turned on the gas fire and hung the shorts over a chair to dry. He would have to iron them in the morning before the match. Ginger, the big tortoiseshell cat, flopped down in front of the fire with her engine going and her tail swishing in gentle ecstasy. For a while they enjoyed each other's company with silent relish, watching the steam rising from the drying shorts.

The warm moisture gave Jim an idea - a hot bath. He looked at his watch. It was late, almost midnight, but he would sleep all the better for it. And so, by the time he had filled the bath, wallowed in it like a grampus, soaped himself three times, tested the way his legs suddenly grew heavier when he lifted them out of the water, measured the length of the hair on his shins, trimmed his toenails with his mother's nail scissors and finally dried himself vigorously, it was past midnight.

But if he thought that Friday the thirteenth had finished with him now, he was very much mistaken. The worst disaster of all was about to happen. He was standing on the bathmat, trying to dry the small of his back by rubbing it against the towel like an itchy horse against a tree, when he heard Ginger coughing. She had run out of the lounge and now stood urgently at the front door, waiting to be let out, retching and coughing like a consumptive chain-smoker.

"Oh, my gosh!" Jim thought. "Fur-balling or biliousness." He suddenly remembered his mother's ominous warning: "If the cat wants to go outside, for heaven's sake don't keep it waiting." He leapt to the front door, swung it back and held open the wrought-iron screen. But with a strange perversity the cat only ran forward a pace or two before coughing and convulsing again.

"Not there! Shoo! Ahh, for Pete's sake!" Jim hastily tied the towel round his waist, flicked off the light switch to avoid being exposed to public view and swept her up in his hands.

"Out you go, whether you like it or not!" He ran across the veranda in his bare feet and tossed her gently on to the garden.

"Off you go! Shoo!"

As he turned to slip back inside again the breeze stirred; the hibiscus swayed by the steps, and the shadows moved in the street lights. Then gently, very gently, the front door swung shut and the latch sprang into the lock with a soft click. Horrified, Jim ran to the door, pushing and heaving. But he was too late. He was locked out. Locked out of his own house, at midnight, and without any clothes on.

For a second or two he cowered, appalled, in the corner of the veranda. But what had seemed so dim and secluded at first soon became more and more exposed as his eyes grew accustomed to the dark. Luckily there was nobody about. The street was deserted, the neighbours were all in bed. Although Jim's mind was still strangely numb, one thought charged about in it like a bull in a yard. He had to get back inside - this instant, before anyone saw him.

His only hope was an unlatched window. He skirted the hibiscus bush in the corner of the garden and made for the dining room. It looked out over the front lawn and held a long view up the curve of the street, but at least there was an off chance that the window there might be unlocked. As he stepped onto the soft grass of the lawn he was astonished to find himself walking on tip-toe. For a second he was vaguely aware of his own tension, a kind of catching himself by surprise before he plunged off across the grass.

For the first three strides the spring of the lawn under his feet was urgently pleasant, but at the fourth step he trod sharply on the garden hose not a foot from the end near the sprinkler, and a squirt of icy water shot out like an electric shock. He leapt up with a noisy gasp and ran to the window. But it was locked. He groaned at the thoroughness of his mother's anti-burglar precautions and stood indecisively for a second, cold drops and runnels of water pausing and chasing down his calves.

Suddenly a car swung into the street and came bearing down on the house, its headlamps boring at him like a searchlight. Too late Jim realised that he was being floodlit like a marble statue in the park, and he flung himself down, commando-style, on the lawn. The car took the curve at speed, and its slashing blade of light swung over him like a scimitar. Jim rose uncertainly to his feet, the soft prickle of the lawn stippling his chest and belly. It was a curiously cold, grassy feeling, but it seemed to salve the hot flush of his embarrassment and shame.

He ran for the other windows along the front of the house, testing each one in turn. They were all locked. Twice more a car raked the house with its headlights, and twice more Jim had to take violent evasive action. The second time, in flinging himself down recklessly behind the espaliered roses, he landed on some old cuttings that his mother had left lying there after her pruning. He only just resisted the impulse to yell and leap up, rolling over on his side in silent agony instead, his fingers trying to seal the cat's-claw scratches down his ribs. The girl in the car turned to her companion enquiringly:

"Darling, what was that thing in the garden there?"

"Dunno. Dog, I s'pose."

"But it looked sort of long and white. Like a pig."

"Ah-h, use your sense, Rosie. How could a white pig be running round the suburbs at this time of night?"

By the time Jim had probed the front and side of the house he was sore and exhausted. But fear drove him on. His only hope now lay in the windows at the back - in the kitchen, laundry and toilet. But these

looked down the steeply sloping back garden where the ground fell away. They were over half a metre beyond his reach. He looked round for a box or stool, but of course his mother was much too careful to have left anything like that lying about the place. Despair began to numb his mind again, just as the creeping goose-pimples on his skin seemed to tighten and contract his body. And then, in a sort of despairing mental lunge, he thought of Mr Hogan's stepladder.

Ben Hogan next door was a good-natured little man who often lent things to the Bears. Jim himself had sometimes borrowed the stepladder from the old shed behind the tank. But there was the problem of getting it out and carrying it back. He couldn't possibly go round by the front gate, without clothes, at this time of night. It would have to be over the back fence - wooden palings two metres high, unpainted and needled all over with long splinters. But a desperate plight called for desperate action.

Happily the two timber cross-pieces that held up the palings were on Jim's side, and he was able to get a foothold on them and swing a leg over the top. Then, with a sudden heave, he hoisted himself up, skinning his calves and thighs, until he was balanced unstably on top. He tied the towel more firmly round his waist and leapt - a kind of dismounting, bucking movement that deposited him on Mrs Hogan's beans with a thud. He quickly disentangled himself and crept over to the woodshed.

For a while it looked as if his luck had changed. The ladder was there right enough, and he managed to half drag, half carry it across to the fence. This time it was going to be a lot easier; he could use the ladder to help himself over.

He stood the steps against the palings and climbed to the top; but here he struck unforeseen trouble, for how was he going to balance himself up there while he transferred the ladder from one side of the fence to the other? He tried squatting down on the paling-tops with one leg on each side, using the cross-bar as a brace for his left foot, but he couldn't get enough leverage that way, and in any case if his foot slipped he had a fair chance of bisecting himself.

He pondered the Archimedean problem, crouched there, riding the fence like a jockey. There was only one thing for it: he would have to stand up to get the extra purchase, and pull the ladder over in seesaw fashion. He jiggled himself along for a metre or so until he reached one of the square wooden posts that held up the fence. There he managed to get himself shakily erect while he slowly turned round for the ladder. But the constant twisting and shuffling was too much for the towel round his middle. As he stood up and heaved, the single knot slipped open suddenly and the towel fell swiftly and silently down into Hogan's garden. And at that moment Mrs Hogan, no less fearful of burglars than Jim's mother, and convinced that she could hear stealthy noises in the back garden, pushed open the screen-door and pointed a rather etiolated beam of torchlight at Jim.

"W . . . who's there?" she demanded, with a queer, quavering truculence. Jim froze. Caught by surprise he could think of nothing more effective to do than to become a statue. A riot of vague pictures from his history lessons tumbled about in his mind - the Elgin marbles, the Laocoön, Hercules . .

He stood stock still, bent forward, naked and precarious on top of the fence, goose-pimples of cold and terror popping out on his buttocks.

Mrs Hogan's yellow torch-beam fell short of him, but a diffused glow caught the fence and endowed Jim with a ghostly lack of substance - a kind of moonlit statuary in suburbia. Mrs Hogan suddenly spotted its vague whiteness and, with a sound that was both gurgle and gasp, retreated in terror. She stumbled to the phone and, after trying to dial with three fingers at once, finally got through to the police.

Meanwhile a scarred and panting Jim, having finished using the paling fence as a pedestal, hastily dragged the ladder into his yard and pushed it against the kitchen window. But when he climbed up to open it at last, the window wouldn't budge. Refusing to believe that it, too, had been locked by his all-suspecting mother, he rattled it furiously. But it held firm. He thumped again with his fists - and then realised with sudden fear that he was making more noise than Macduff knocking at the gates in Inverness. He shrank away from the window and crept down the ladder again. A spasm of shivering swept over him, and his teeth chattered.

Then he saw something. Standing upright in his father's potato patch was a four-pronged garden fork - the perfect lever to wedge in under the stubborn window. He ran over, dragged it from the ground and climbed back up the ladder. It was fairly easy to push the points of the prongs into the narrow slit between the frame and the window, but in his eagerness he didn't wedge them in far enough, so that when he bore down heavily on the handle, the tines suddenly splintered out of the wood and he all but dived headlong on to the gravel below. He saved himself by a frenzied and lucky clutch at the sill while the fork gonged like a bass tuning-fork against the concrete foundations beneath.

Jim hung there breathless for a second, but a spark of hope still glimmered with the moonshine on the tines. He descended, picked up the fork and returned to the attack. This time he would make sure that he had the maximum possible purchase without the wood giving way. Twice he drove the tines in with what strength he could, but each time as he pressed down tentatively on the handle he felt them slipping out again. It would need a sudden vicious jab. He swung back and thrust the fork in sharply like a bayonet. But there were four points instead of one, and somehow the fork seemed to turn in his hand as he thrust. There was a grating crack, a clash of falling fragments as one of the tines struck glass instead of wood, and the window gaped emptily in front of him. Jim stared at it unbelievingly. Then he laughed - a sobbing laugh of incredulity and relief. For there was the opening! All he had to do was to crawl through it to safety and peace. In the morning he could get a pane of glass, fit it with tacks and putty and there it was. Who would ever know?

A car raced up the street and stopped. Doors opened and footsteps hurried about the paths. Some went into Hogan's next door, and there was the sound of low and urgent consultation. Jim, still clutching the fork, crouched in the shadow on top of his ladder. The voices stopped and more footsteps crunched on the gravel. Some came over towards the fence and Jim froze against the wall in terror. Then, quite suddenly, a strong beam of light flashed onto him, and two policemen stood in the drive below.

"There he is!"

"Look out!"

"Move in slowly!"

"Watch that fork!"

Jim made a strangled sound as the policemen slowly moved in, never dousing the merciless glare of their torches for an instant. It didn't occur to him that a naked young man brandishing a digging fork on top of a ladder at midnight would scarcely look either modest or peace-loving. He felt ruthlessly exposed, a violent sense of intrusion, and tried unsuccessfully to hide behind the handle of the fork. At the same time he knew it was essential to say something reassuring, to explain the whole business simply and clearly. But the best he could manage was "I ... I ..." Two more policemen joined in the blockade and all four closed in steadily. They didn't say a word. Jim's mouth went on working until suddenly he surprised himself by announcing in a high squeak: "Look here, I'm Bear! Jim Bear!" The policemen either silently agreed or took it as a threat. For with a sudden rush they swept him from the ladder, flung off the fork and bundled him unceremoniously on his back in the strawberry patch.

"Grab him!"

But at that moment Jim came violently to life. He leapt to his feet and sped round the house like a gazelle. The heavy sergeant pounded after him, and two of the younger policemen ran up the drive to try to head him off. But Jim had a clear lead. He shot across the lawn, took the front fence at a stride, and raced out on to the street almost under the wheels of a car. He and the car swerved simultaneously. There was a shriek of a woman and a screeching of tyres.

"It's him!" the woman screamed. "It's the burglar!" There was a second of confusion as the police were cut off by the swerving driver. It was enough to give him the advantage. He swung back on to the footpath, hurdled Schuberts' fence next door, shot across their lawn, hurtled through two back gardens, then doubled back and crouched behind the creeper that sprawled along his own back fence. Luckily at the same moment a dog barked further up the street. It unwittingly acted as a decoy, and the footsteps and voices of his pursuers faded away hurriedly towards it.

Jim stood up cautiously and listened. No sound.

He peered over the fence into the back garden. No sign. The stepladder still stood by the gaping kitchen window and the fork shone dimly in the garden strip below. Up to this point in his flight he had acted wholly by reflex and instinct; from the moment the policemen had appeared below him he hadn't planned so much as a gesture. But now his mind began working again, craftily. Doubling back on his tracks to outwit his pursuers had been good strategy. He had often seen it done on TV, so why not in real life?

Stealthily he hauled himself over the back fence and dropped down into his own back garden. There he paused, breathing cautiously. No sound or movement. With sudden resolution he tiptoed across the back lawn, leapt the strawberry patch, ran lightly up the stepladder and eased himself in through the broken window. The whole thing only took a couple of seconds. From the sill he lowered himself noiselessly inside, stepped gingerly for a metre or two, trying to avoid treading on broken glass, and then hurried down the darkness of the passage. His pyjamas were hanging on the bathroom rail. He put them on with a kind of breathless haste, the touch of clothing against his flesh suddenly filling him with a strange sense of security and gratitude. Then he padded quickly up to his room, got into bed and pulled the bedclothes high up round his shoulders.

7.3 **Into Film.**

Imagine that the story is being turned into a short film for television. In groups of four or five, work through the following activities, keeping a record of all the decisions you make.

1 The story begins at eleven o'clock at night. On a piece of paper each individual in the group should write down what time they think the story ends (i.e. when Jim goes back to bed) to the exact minute. Compare results and try to decide who has given the most likely time. You will find that the discussion will make you more familiar with the story. How long should you allow for the television film?

2 The action takes place mainly in one location. Draw a diagram of the set which would have to be built or found to film the story. Label the diagram and make sure you include the fences, windows, lawn, Hogan's shed, position of car.

3 ☆ You have decided that in the whole film you will use just six close-up shots of Jim's face to show his expression at key points. Otherwise you will use medium and long shots. Choose the most appropriate moments in the story for the close-ups. Identify the moment precisely by quoting the words from the text and giving a description of Jim's expression. Remember to use inverted commas for quotations from the text.

Long shot.

Medium shot.

Close-up.

"The warm moisture gave Jim an idea - a hot bath"

Look at the illustrations which accompany the story and then look at **A** which shows an event from the story in a very different way. The first drawings give a humorous interpretation while **A** stresses the unpleasant side of the whole experience showing Jim's fear and discomfort more than anything else.

A director can interpret a text in different ways.

4 Select five scenes from the story and describe how a director might deal with each scene in two different ways, one to make it seem more humorous and the other to stress the fear and nastiness. Even the point at which Jim drops the towel could be made to seem serious if his face showed desperation.

Scene.	Development 1.	Development 2.
"....he landed on some old cuttings that his mother had left lying there after pruning..."	Lands on thorns - jumps up grabbing his behind, making a face. Puts his hand to the left and places that in some thorns. Mouths "ouch" silently and puts his hand under his armpit to ease sting.	Lands on the thorns - seem to encircle him as he falls on them. Close-up of scratches on his chest as he tries to get up. Groans in pain - starts to rise. A branch clings to him and blood has started to appear on his side. Rubs side and looks at it - makes a face showing obvious pain.

5 How would different lighting, music, and back-ground setting change the tone from humour to one of suspense and fear?

Now try ......

6 Back at the station one of the police officers stopped off in the tea room and told his friend what had happened. His account went something like this:

"Well we've had a right carry on tonight. I mean really, it was just daft. You see like we got this call from an old dear who said she's seen a bloke with no clothes on in the garden. Well, I should say. We didn't really believe her but we was round there in a jiff and blimey she was telling the truth. This geezer parading round he was - must have been trying to break in starkers. You wouldn't believe it. Well we tackled him but he legged it and that was it. Where he went without a stitch on I don't know. We come straight back here."

After his cup of tea, the same officer had to write a written report of the incident. In pairs, discuss the verbal account above and say what aspects of it which, although fine when speaking informally, would be inappropriate for a formal written report.

7 Now write the report which was written by the officer.

8 When Mrs. Hogan spotted Jim in the garden she telephoned the police. At first she was in a panic. She started off as follows, "Help, come quickly... he's in the garden.... please.... quickly.... I've seen him..... he might come here.... no clothes.... " When the police calmed her down she produced a more helpful report. Write out her version of events.

9 In the newspaper the story becomes completely exaggerated and sensationalized. Write the headline and article.

7.4 Questions To Ask?

Why Me?

When dad found a snail in his slipper
And mum found a slug in her tea
And my sister Sue
Found her comb smeared with glue
Why did they think it was me?

When Auntie May dropped in for coffee
And found that it tasted of salt
And the cake that she tried
Had a rat's tail inside
Why did she think it my fault?

When our teacher got hit by a snowball
He certainly wasn't amused
The cold made him wiggle
We started to giggle
And I was the one he accused.

When our class was at morning assembly
And the Headteacher called out my name
And a voice from the front
Made a terrible grunt
Why was it I got the blame?

When I heard a loud exclamation
"Jane you've really gone too far this time!"
By the tone of the voice
I knew I'd no choice
But to listen to my latest crime.

Chris Evans

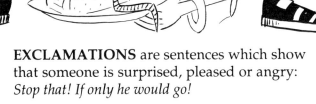

 REMINDER - Questions.

You will notice that each question is followed by a question mark in the poem. Make sure you always use question marks in your work. It is easy to forget them. Questions are usually easy to spot but sometimes a statement is turned into a question by the use of a questioning tone of voice. Read these statements aloud:
Jim is naked.
Jim is naked?
What is the difference?

RHETORICAL questions are ones to which you do not expect an answer:
Who cares? Will you be quiet?

EXCLAMATIONS are sentences which show that someone is surprised, pleased or angry:
Stop that! If only he would go!

Sometimes sentences can look like questions, but they are actually exclamations:
Wasn't that a great meal!
Notice that the poem has one exclamation and several questions.

(1) Try writing your own humorous poem which ends each verse with a question,
"Why is it always me?" or *"Why me?"*.
It is up to you whether you make it rhyme or not.

Note Taking.

Have you ever been accused of something that you did not do?
In pairs, interview each other about the incident and take notes as your partner replies but try not to slow down the interview too much.
If you cannot ever remember being wrongly accused you may invent an incident or use one which has happened to a friend.

Here are some questions to ask.

When did the incident happen?
Where did it take place?
What were you supposed to have done?
Who was the guilty one?
Who blamed you for what happened?
How did you react at the time?
How did you feel?

When you have finished taking notes retell the incident to your partner and see how much of the detail you managed to recall.

When?

Where?

Event?

Responsibility?

Feelings?

Skimming for information.

We are not given a single detailed description of the area in which Jim lives but we can work this out from different clues given in different parts of the story.

Describe what sort of area it is. You will need to re-read parts of the story. Try skimming the story to find the relevant parts. Let your eye travel fairly quickly over the page while watching out for relevant information. It takes some practice.

Now try . . . . . .

2 All the way through the story we are given information about the way Jim is feeling by the author's careful use of words and phrases. Write down as many words as you can find which tell us about the way he is feeling at different parts of the story and discuss your choice with a friend.

3 Jim's mother and father arrive back earlier than expected the next morning to find the broken window. Jim has some difficulty convincing them of the truth. Write out the conversation they had in play form.

4 You have thought about turning the story into a television film. Would it make a radio play? There is very little speech and that would present a major problem. Sometimes the problem is overcome on the radio by having the character speak his thoughts. Rewrite the last two paragraphs of the story in the first person rather than the third person and in the present rather than the past tense so that you are conveying the information as if these are Jim's thoughts. You will need to change some of the detail, e.g.

"I'll just stand up and listen. It's absolutely quiet. They must have gone..."

You have probably written and read about animals before, but in this unit we hope you will think carefully about what animals are really like. You will therefore find emphasis on observing animals closely. You will also be thinking about adjectives and adverbs.

(1) ☆ Here are sixteen statements about animals. Thirteen of them are true; three of them are false. In pairs, decide which of the statements are true and which are false. If you think any are false try to give your reasons.

Now try . . . . . .

2 Do some research and try to make your own list of ten statements about animals in order to test the class or group. When you invent statements make sure they are not too ridiculous.

1 Fireflies are not flies and glow worms are not worms.

2 A mole sometimes ties a worm in a knot in order to keep it for eating later.

3 A sloth sleeps for about 20 hours out of every 24.

4 Rabbits rub their chins on sticks so that they do not grow beards.

5 If a female common frog is kept at an even temperature of 26.6 degrees centigrade it will turn into a male.

6 An earless lizard can live for a day without breathing oxygen.

7 A goat never falls asleep properly.

8 It is thought that a New Zealand tuatara lizard can live for 300 years.

9 If you took a kangaroo for a hop around town you could be fined for speeding.

10 A camel has been known to drink 50 gallons of water in 10 minutes.

11 A rabbit living close to a fox is less likely to be eaten by the fox than one living some way away.

12 Harvest mice have been known to toast grain by the embers of a bonfire before eating it.

13 A basilisk lizard can run on water.

14 Chimpanzees make and use toothpicks.

15 Humpback whales can hear each other at distances of hundreds of miles.

16 The so-called "reverse-fish" swims backwards so that it can see if it is being chased.

(You can find the answers on page 96.)

When he was a boy, Gerald Durrell spent a lot of time looking very closely at animals. He wanted to find out everything he could about them, and so he noticed tiny details. In his writing you will notice how carefully he uses adjectives and adverbs. A gecko is a small lizard. Pads on its feet enable it to walk upside down on ceilings. This particular gecko used to come into Gerald Durrell's bedroom every night. It used his ceiling as a hunting ground and was called Geronimo by the Durrell family.

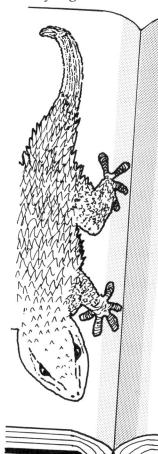

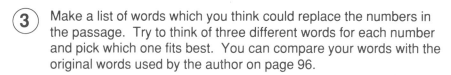

Watching Geronimo's stalking tactics was quite an education. A lacewing or a moth, having spun round the lamp until it was dizzy, would flutter up and settle on the ceiling in the white circle of lamplight printed there. Geronimo, hanging upside down in his corner, would stiffen. He would nod his head two or three times very rapidly and then start to edge across the ceiling ....1...., milimetre by milimetre, his ....2.... eyes on the insect in a fixed stare. ....3...., he would slide over the plaster until he was six inches or so away from his prey, whereupon he stopped for a second and you could see his padded toes moving as he made his grip on the plaster more secure. His eyes would become more protuberant with excitement, what he imagined to be a look of blood-curdling ferocity would spread over his face, the tip of his tail would twitch minutely, and then he would skim across the ceiling as ....4.... as a drop of water, there would be a faint snap, and he would turn around, an expression of smug happiness on his face, the lacewing inside his mouth with its legs and wings trailing over his lips like a strange, quivering walrus moustache. He would wag his tail vigorously, like an ....5.... puppy, and then trot back to his resting place to consume his meal in comfort.

Now try . . . . . .

3 Make a list of words which you think could replace the numbers in the passage. Try to think of three different words for each number and pick which one fits best. You can compare your words with the original words used by the author on page 96.

4 Durrell does not just tell us what happens. We can imagine the gecko because he uses exact words to describe what he means. He uses vivid adjectives like "blood-curdling" and precise adverbs like "minutely". Imagine that you are giving a talk about what Gerald Durrell has just described to a group of people who are interested in animals. You are going to use six slides or photographs to illustrate your talk. Draw the six most useful "frames" and write a sentence or two under each to explain what is happening in each picture.

5 In a group or as a class, choose one person to send away (Person A). The rest must choose an ADVERB (e.g. CAREFULLY). Person A then tells the rest to perform various activities (e.g. to brush the floor). The rest do whatever they are told AS DESCRIBED BY THE ADVERB. The aim is for Person A to guess the chosen adverb. You can repeat this activity until everyone has had their turn.

Animal Behaviour.

1 Either study the picture of an animal on this page or choose an animal you know well. Make a list of adjectives that describe it as exactly as possible. Next, make a list of adverbs that describe how it moves. Then write two paragraphs, the first describing your animal when it is still, and the second describing it when it is moving.

2 Watch an animal - any will do - for two minutes exactly. Note down every movement of the animal during those two minutes. Then write down as exactly as you can what the animal did - as Gerald Durrell has with the gecko. Even a sleeping dog will make many movements in two minutes. Can you suggest any reason for its movements?

Now try . . . . . .

3 You will need to be in a small group for this activity. Every member of the group has to tell the others a story about an animal doing something unusual. For example you could tell the story of a kitten that adopted a dog as its mother! Plan your story carefully so that it is interesting and convincing.
FIRST: Quickly make a list of the important events in your story.
SECOND: Arrange them in an order which you think is the best.
THEN: Tell your story to interest your listener as much as you can.
The rest of the group have to guess whether each story is true or false.

4 What makes a good story?
You could discuss the differences between your story and the others in the group in order to decide. Each group could then choose one of the stories to tell to the rest of the class.

5 Make a class collection of true stories of unusual animal behaviour. These may be things you have seen or heard about, or you may research stories in the library. Remember to suggest reasons for the behaviour.

ANIMAL COMMUNICATION

Before you think about the ways in which animals communicate (that is, tell each other what they mean), think about human communication. One way we communicate is by what we say, but we also use other methods.

6 **Facial expression.** Draw six very simple pictures of a face (with just eyes, nose, mouth and hair) showing surprise, happiness, sadness, embarrassment, anger and fear. Write a caption to go with each drawing. In the example someone has just eaten something sour. Ugh!

7 **Tone of voice.** In pairs read the following sentences in three different ways to make them mean something different each time. "Are you going with Michael to the pictures?" "I'm going on holiday next year if mum lets me." You will notice that you have to put stress on different words to change the meaning. Now read the following dialogue in two different ways, first with A being meek and rather apologetic for being late and then with A being fairly angry.

B *It's already five past nine. You're rather late you know.*
A *It wasn't my fault. The bus was late.*
B *You'll have to arrive earlier in future.*
A *I couldn't help it. I'm not usually late. This is the first time this term.*

Animals communicate by using sounds, signs and gestures. It is obvious what these young birds mean. Some animals have developed quite complicated "vocabularies", using sounds, signs and gestures. We do not understand them all, but there is always a meaning if we look for it. A strange dog will make it quite clear whether he is going to be friendly or not. Some animals find mates in bizarre ways. A North American firefly attracts females by flashing a light in his body every six seconds. The female matches this by flashing her light exactly two seconds after this.

Birds warn each other of danger by calls which are quite different from their usual songs.

If a honeybee has found nectar it needs to tell the other bees. It does this by performing a "waggle dance" which tells the others exactly where the nectar is - its direction and how far away it is.

(1) Very often the way an animal behaves tells us what it is "thinking" or "feeling". In pairs, think of ways in which certain animals might behave when they are:
(a) frightened   (b) hungry
(c) content   (d) angry.
The words "feeling" and "thinking" have been put in inverted commas because it is not certain whether it is right to use those terms when speaking about animals.
What do you think?

Now try . . . . . .

2 Do some research and find out as much as you can about different forms of communication between animals, e.g. What does it mean when chimpanzees "groom" each other?
Choose a particular animal and find out as much as you can about it. Write this up and include pictures - photographs or drawings.

Have you ever thought how much we insult animals by the language we use? Think about the different expressions people use as insults. *"You clumsy ox!" "This place is like a pigsty!"* *"You're eating like a pig."* *"You cheeky monkey." "You little worm!"* Of course many expressions we use which include animals are not insults, for example, *"He is eagle-eyed,"* meaning someone can see well or is perceptive.

③ Think of as many expressions as you can which describe people by referring to an animal. In each say whether you think the expression seems to make sense. In other words - are animals really like that?

④ ☆ People have different opinions about zoos. Some argue that zoos are important because they keep species alive which would otherwise be extinct; others argue that they are cruel and unnatural. Imagine that there is pressure to close down a zoo which is in your area. Write a short speech which you would give at a meeting arguing for or against the proposal.

⑤ Design a poster which either supports or opposes the proposal to close the zoo.

⑥ Imagine that the eventual decision is to improve the zoo rather than close it down. Draw a labelled diagram which shows your design for the ideal zoo. Money is no object!

Animal Poems.

Hedgehog

Twitching the leaves just where the drainpipe clogs
In ivy leaves and mud, a purposeful
Creature at night about its business. Dogs
Fear his stiff seriousness. He chews away

At beetles, worms, slugs, frogs. Can kill a hen
With one snap of his jaws, can taunt a snake
To death on muscled spines. Old countrymen
Tell tales of hedgehogs sucking a cow dry.

But this one, cramped by houses, fences, walls,
Must have slept here all winter in that heap
Of compost, or have inched by intervals
Through tidy gardens to this ivy bed.

And here, dim-eyed, but ears so sensitive
A voice within the house can make him freeze,
He scuffs the edge of danger; yet can live
Happily in our nights and absences.

A country creature, wary, quiet, and shrewd,
He takes the milk we give to him, when we're gone.
At night; our slamming voices must seem crude
To one who sits and waits for silences.

Anthony Thwaite

(1) Draw a table like this:

The character of a hedgehog	What it eats	What it does	What other animals think of it	How it differs from people

(2) Using only what the poem tells you, write notes in each column. Then discuss in class what you have under each heading.

(3) The poem uses a number of adjectives. Choose three which you think add most to the poem. Try replacing those words with others which are much less effective:
e.g. At night, our *slamming* voices..   At night, our *loud* voices......
By doing that, you will see how careful poets are when they choose words.

(4) Choose another animal and, using the same five columns as for the hedgehog, write down notes about your animal. Then, using your notes, prepare a piece of writing that captures the character of your animal. This may be a poem if you wish.

Some Japanese poems are very short - just 17 syllables in 3 lines. Two different forms of Japanese poems, both of which contain only 17 syllables, are a HAIKU and a SENRYU. In order to write a poem of only 17 syllables, you must choose every word very carefully.

A common pattern for such a poem is to have 5 syllables in the first and third lines, and 7 syllables in the second line. This makes the pattern:- 5 - 7 - 5.

Here is an example:

> The cuckoo's note hangs
> Sweetly in the still June trees.
> Fruit to be devoured.

Such poems do not need to rhyme. As you will see from the other poems on this page, not all such poems have exactly 17 syllables in exactly that pattern.

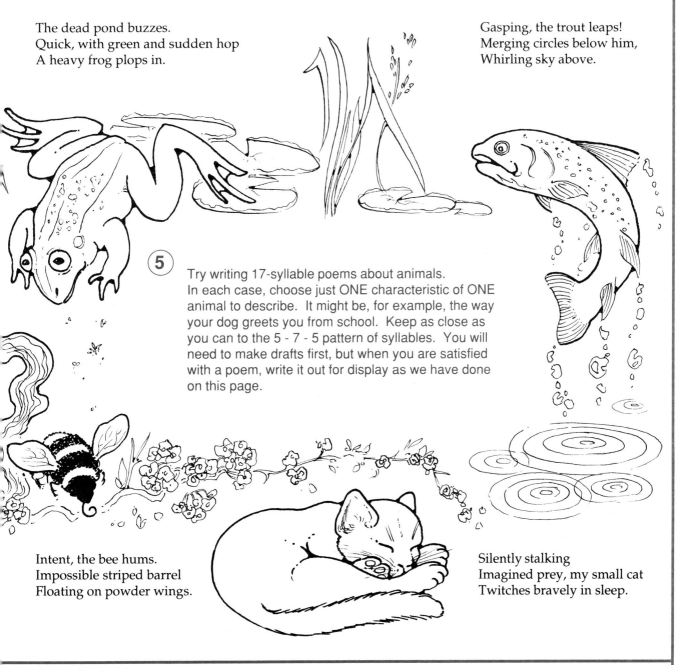

The dead pond buzzes.
Quick, with green and sudden hop
A heavy frog plops in.

Gasping, the trout leaps!
Merging circles below him,
Whirling sky above.

(5) Try writing 17-syllable poems about animals. In each case, choose just ONE characteristic of ONE animal to describe. It might be, for example, the way your dog greets you from school. Keep as close as you can to the 5 - 7 - 5 pattern of syllables. You will need to make drafts first, but when you are satisfied with a poem, write it out for display as we have done on this page.

Intent, the bee hums.
Impossible striped barrel
Floating on powder wings.

Silently stalking
Imagined prey, my small cat
Twitches bravely in sleep.

Ways of Seeing.

In this unit you will be reading a story about a man who can see without his eyes and will also explore ways in which we can be made to see things in different ways.

Read the following passage from Roald Dahl's *"The Wonderful Story of Henry Sugar"*.

I, John Cartwright, am a surgeon at Bombay General Hospital. On the morning of the second of December, 1934, I was in the doctors' rest room having a cup of tea.

There were three other doctors there with me, all having a well earned tea break. They were Dr. Marshall, Dr. Phillips and Dr. Macfarlane. There was a knock on the door. "Come in," I said.

The door opened and an Indian came in and smiled at us and said, "Excuse me, please. Could I ask you gentlemen a favour?"

The doctors' rest room was a most private place. Nobody other than a doctor was allowed to enter it except in an emergency.

"This is a private room," Dr. Macfarlane said sharply.

"Yes, yes," he answered. "I know that and I am very sorry to be bursting in like this, sirs, but I have a most interesting thing to show you."

All four of us were pretty annoyed and we didn't say anything.

"Gentlemen," he said. "I am a man who can see without using his eyes."

We still didn't invite him to go on. But we didn't kick him out either.

"You can cover my eyes in any way you wish," he said. "You can bandage my head with fifty bandages and I will still be able to read you a book."

He seemed perfectly serious. I felt my curiosity beginning to stir.

"Come here," I said. He came over to me. "Turn around." He turned around. I placed my hands firmly over his eyes, holding the lids closed. "Now," I said, "one of the doctors in the room is going to hold up some fingers. Tell me how many he is holding up."

Dr. Marshall held up seven fingers.

"Seven," the Indian said.

"Once more," I said.

Dr. Marshall clenched both fists and hid all his fingers.

"No fingers," the Indian said.

I removed my hands from his eyes. "Not bad," I said.

"Hold on," Dr. Marshall said. "Let's try this." There was a doctor's white coat hanging from a peg on the door. Dr. Marshall took it down and rolled it into a sort of long scarf. He then wound it round the Indian's head and held the ends tight at the back.

"Try him now," Dr. Marshall said. I took a key from my pocket.

"What is this?" I asked.

"A key," he answered.

I put the key back and held up an empty hand. "What is this object?" I asked him.

"There isn't any object," the Indian said. "Your hand is empty."

Dr. Marshall removed the covering from the man's eyes. "How do you do it?" he asked. "What's the trick?"

"There is no trick," the Indian said. "It is a genuine thing that I have managed after years of training."

"What sort of training?" I asked.

"Forgive me, sir," he said, "but that is a private matter."

"Then why did you come here?" I asked.

"I came to request a favour of you," he said.

The Indian was a tall man of about thirty with light brown skin the colour of coconut. He had a small black moustache. Also, there was a curious matting of black hair growing all over the outsides of his ears. He wore a white cotton robe, and had sandals on his bare feet.

"You see, gentlemen," he went on. "I am at present earning my living by working in a travelling theatre, and we have just arrived here in Bombay. Tonight we give our opening performance."

"Where do you give it?" I asked.

"In the Royal Palace Hall," he answered. "In Acacia Street. I am the star performer. I am billed on the programme as 'Imhrat Khan, the man who sees without his eyes,' and it is my duty to advertise the show in a big way. If we do not sell tickets, we don't eat."

"What does this have to do with us?" I asked him.

"Very interesting for you," he said. "Lots of fun. Let me explain. You see, whenever our theatre arrives in a new town, I myself go straight to the largest hospital and I ask the doctors there to bandage my eyes. I ask them to do it in the most expert fashion. They must make sure that my eyes are completely covered many times over. It is important that this job is done by doctors, otherwise people will think I am cheating. Then, when I am fully bandaged, I go out into the street and I do a dangerous thing."

"What do you mean by that?" I asked.

"What I mean is that I do something that is extremely dangerous for someone who cannot see."

"What do you do?" I asked.

"It is very interesting," he said. "And you will see me do it if you will be so kind as to bandage me up first. It would be a great favour to me if you will do this little thing, sirs."

I looked at the other three doctors. Dr. Phillips said he had to go back to his patients. Dr. Macfarlane said the same.

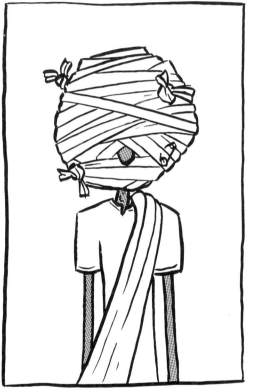

Dr. Marshall said, "Well, why not? It might be amusing. It won't take a minute."

"I'm with you," I said. "But let's do the job properly. Let's make absolutely sure he can't peep."

"You are extremely kind," the Indian said. "Please do whatever you wish."

Dr. Phillips and Dr. Macfarlane left the room.

"Before we bandage him," I said to Dr. Marshall, "let's first seal down his eyelids. When we've done that, we'll fill his sockets with something soft and solid and sticky."

"Such as what?" Dr. Marshall asked.

"What about dough?"

"Dough would be perfect," Dr. Marshall said.

"Right," I said. "If you will nip down to the hospital bakery and get some dough, I'll take him

into the surgery and seal his lids."

I led the Indian out of the rest room and down the long hospital corridor to the surgery. "Lie down there," I said, indicating the high bed. He lay down. I took a small bottle from the cupboard. It had an eyedropper in the top. "This is something called colodion," I told him. "It will harden over your closed eyelids so that it is impossible for you to open them."

"How do I get it off afterward?" he asked me.

"Alcohol will dissolve it away quite easily," I said. "It's perfectly harmless. Close your eyes now."

The Indian closed his eyes. I applied the colodion to both lids. "Keep them closed," I said. "Wait for it to harden."

In a couple of minutes, the colodion had made a hard film over the eyelids, sticking them down tight. "Try to open them," I said.

He tried but couldn't.

Dr. Marshall came in with a basin of dough. It was the ordinary white dough used for baking bread. It was nice and soft. I took a lump of the dough and plastered it over one of the Indian's eyes. I filled the whole socket and let the dough overlap onto the surrounding skin. Then I pressed the edges down hard. I did the same with the other eye.

"That isn't too uncomfortable, is it?" I asked.

"No," said the Indian. "It's fine."

"You do the bandaging," I said to Dr. Marshall. "My fingers are too sticky."

"A pleasure," Dr. Marshall said. "Watch this." He took a thick wad of cotton wool and laid it on top of the Indian's dough-filled eyes. The cotton wool stuck to the dough and stayed in place. "Sit down, please," Dr. Marshall said.

The Indian sat on the bed.

Dr. Marshall took a roll of three-inch bandage and proceeded to wrap it round and round the man's head. The bandage held the cotton wool and dough firmly in place. Dr. Marshall pinned the bandage. After that, he took a second bandage and began to wrap that one not only around the man's eyes but around his entire face and head.

"Please leave my nose free for breathing," the

"Of course," Dr. Marshall answered. He finished the job and pinned down the end of the bandage. "How's that?" he asked.

"Splendid," I said. "There's no way he can possibly see through that."
Indian said.

The whole of the Indian's head was now swathed in thick white bandage, and the only thing you could see was the end of the nose sticking out. He looked like a man who had had some terrible brain operation.

"How does that feel?" Dr. Marshall asked him.

"It feels good," the Indian said. "I must compliment you gentlemen on doing such a fine job."

"Off you go, then," Dr. Marshall said, grinning at me. "Show us how clever you are at seeing things now."

The Indian got off the bed and walked straight to the door. He opened the door and went out.

"Great Scott!" I said. "Did you see that? He put his hand right on the doorknob?"

Dr. Marshall had stopped grinning. His face had suddenly gone white. "I'm going after him," he said rushing for the door. I rushed for the door as well. The Indian was walking quite normally along the hospital corridor. Dr. Marshall and I were about five yards behind him. And very spooky it was to watch this man with the enormous white and totally bandaged head strolling casually along the corridor just like anyone else. It was especially spooky when you knew for a certainty that his eyelids were sealed, that his eye sockets were filled with dough, and that there was a great wad of cotton wool and bandages on top of that.

I saw a native orderly coming along the corridor toward the Indian. He was pushing a food trolley. Suddenly the orderly caught sight of the man with the white head, and he froze. The bandaged Indian stepped casually to one side of the trolley and went on.

"He saw it!" I cried. "He must have seen that trolley! He walked right round it! This is absolutely unbelievable!"

Dr. Marshall didn't answer me. His cheeks were white, his whole face rigid with shocked disbelief. The Indian came to the stairs and started to go down them. He went down with no trouble at all. He didn't even put a hand on the handrail. Several people were coming up the stairs. Each of them stopped, stared and quickly got out of the way.

At the bottom of the stairs, the Indian turned right and headed for the doors that led into the street. Dr. Marshall and I kept close behind him.

The entrance to our hospital stands back a little

from the street, and there is a rather grand series of steps leading down from the entrance into a small courtyard with acacia trees around it. Dr. Marshall and I came out into the blazing sunshine and stood at the top of the steps. Below us, in the courtyard, we saw a crowd of maybe a hundred people. At least half of them were barefoot children, and as our white-headed Indian walked down the steps, they all cheered and shouted and surged toward him. He greeted them by holding both hands above his head.

Suddenly I saw the bicycle. It was over to one side at the bottom of the steps, and a small boy was holding it. The bicycle itself was quite ordinary, but on the back of it, fixed somewhere to the rear wheel frame, was a huge placard, about five feet square.

On the placard were written the following words:

**Imhrat Khan,
The Man Who Sees Without His Eyes!
Today my eyes have been bandaged by
hospital doctors!
Appearing Tonight and all this week at
The Royal Palace Hall, Acacia Street,
at 7 P.M.
Don't miss it!
You will see miracles performed!**

Our Indian had reached the bottom of the steps and now he walked straight over to his bicycle. He said something to the boy, and the boy smiled. The Indian mounted the bicycle. The crowd made way for him. Then, lo and behold, this fellow with the blocked-up bandaged eyes now proceeded to ride across the courtyard and straight out into the bustling honking traffic of the street beyond!

The crowd cheered louder than ever. The barefoot children ran after him squealing and laughing. For a minute or so we were able to keep him in sight. We saw him riding superbly down the busy street with cars whizzing past him and a bunch of children running after his wake. Then he turned a corner and was gone.

"I feel quite giddy," Dr. Marshall said. "I can't bring myself to believe it."

"We have to believe it," I said. "He couldn't possibly have removed the dough from under the bandages. We never let him out of our sight. And as for unsealing his eyelids, that job would take him five minutes with cotton wool and alcohol."

"Do you know what I think," Dr. Marshall said. "I think we have just witnessed a miracle."

We turned and walked slowly back into the hospital.

 REMINDER - Pronouns.

In both speaking and writing we use pronouns all the time in place of nouns. They are useful because they add variety to sentences. Without pronouns the previous sentence would have been written *"Pronouns are useful because pronouns add variety to sentences"* - which is very repetitive.

The story is made to sound real partly because it is written in the first person; that is, it is written from the point of view of Mr Cartwright (using *"I"*) as if he is telling the story. Copy out the first paragraph of the story changing it from first person to third person. Begin as follows: *"John Cartwright is a surgeon at Bombay Hospital. On the morning of the second of December, 1934 he was ..... "*

Now try . . . . . .

1. Imagine that as soon as he went back to his office, John Cartwright wrote notes on which he would later base this story. Write out the three lists he might have made to record (a) the exact test they gave the Indian before they bandaged his eyes, (b) the steps they took when they were completely sealing and covering his eyes, and (c) the different things the Indian did from the moment his eyes were fully bandaged to show that he could see.

2. Dr. Cartwright actually goes to see the show which was advertised. Describe what he sees. Write it as if you are the doctor. You could start as follows: *"That evening I made my way to the Royal Palace Hotel in Acacia Street to see the show. It started at exactly 7.00 p.m. This is what I saw..."*

3. This is just a story but the writer makes it sound real by describing everything in such detail. Before the Indian has his eyes completely sealed he could have been tricking the doctors. Can you think of a way in which he might have been tricking them?

4. Imagine that two of the doctors are interviewed on the radio that evening. In groups of three conduct the interview.

5. Can you think of any other unusual powers possessed by humans which you have heard or read about? In each case say whether the power is supposed to be true, for example people who can walk on fire, or just fiction, for example the powers of "superheroes" like Superman.

6. You might like to read the complete story by Roald Dahl for yourself. In the story Henry Sugar learns to see through solid material. What do you think he uses the power for?

9.2 **Illusions.**

Magicians create illusions. They make us believe we are seeing things which cannot really be happening. A famous illusion is created when a magician places someone inside a box and seems to place a number of swords through the person's body. Here is a description of how that trick could be done, using cardboard sticks instead of swords, for safety reasons!

THE DISAPPEARING COIN

66 You ask your assistant to step into a large box. When he or she has done so, he turns so that he is actually sitting sideways, but the audience thinks that he or she is still facing them. You can then slowly push ten cardboard swords from different directions into the box. When you remove them, your assistant can stand up showing he/she is unharmed. 99

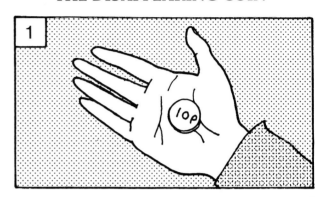

(1) Imagine that you are editing a book on Magical Tricks and Illusions. You want to include this trick, but you want to make it much clearer and you need to use the headings which you are using for other tricks in the book.
Rewrite the trick in careful stages using the following headings:
(1) WHAT YOU WILL NEED
(2) PREPARATION
(3) THE SECRET
(4) PERFORMING THE TRICK
(Write the method out in a list of numbered stages).

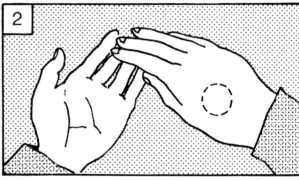

Note that when you are writing instructions of this kind you have to be careful with your use of pronouns so that the reader understands what you mean. For example, if you write:
"You have a glass and a coin in front of you. Pick it up ...", it is not clear to what "it" refers.

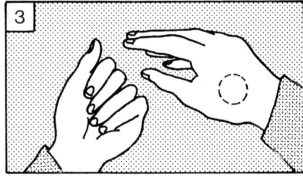

(2) Write simple instructions to go with the diagrams of the simple magic trick shown on this page.

(3) Do you know any magic tricks? Write out instructions explaining clearly how to perform them and give your explanation to someone else in the class to see if they can follow the instructions. Keep your language simple and direct. Write in simple sentences.

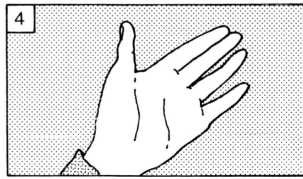

TELEPATHY

The term "telepathy" is used when it appears that people are communicating with each other's minds without speaking or using any obvious signs. Magicians sometimes give the impression that they are using telepathy. For example, the magician's assistant is given a number while the magician is out of the room. When he returns he places his hands on the assistant's temples and without any other communication is able to repeat the number. The secret is that the assistant is able to communicate the number by clenching his teeth the appropriate number of times without the audience realising what is happening. The magician can feel the movement through his fingers. However there are cases reported which are not simply tricks performed by magicians. At the precise moment a man crashed his car, his young son at the breakfast table said , "Dad's in trouble." A girl claimed to feel sudden terrible pain in her hand and later found out that her twin many miles away had burned herself at precisely the same time. Sometimes people can tell exactly what someone is about to say before they have said it. Perhaps these are all just simple coincidences.

4 **A** shows a photograph of a test for telepathy. Describe what you think is happening.

5 Coincidence or special powers? What are your views on such matters? Write what you think in a paragraph.

6 Try carrying out tests on each other similar to the one shown in the photograph. Keep a check on how many right answers you get, and write up your findings. Does anyone in the class achieve results markedly different from everyone else?

LOOK AGAIN

Look at these pictures. What can you see in them?

9.3 Seeing Pictures.

Look at these four shapes. Are they simply ink blots or can you see "pictures" in them?

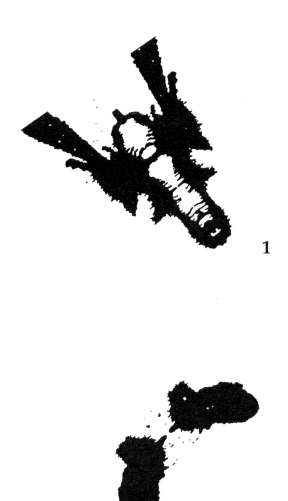

1

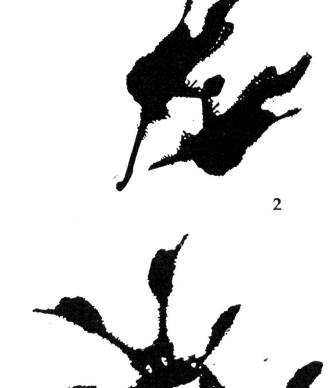

2

3

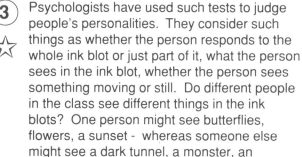

4

① Describe the different objects and scenes you can "see" in each of the pictures 1 to 4. Try to be as imaginative as you can. List your ideas under the heading INK BLOTS and you will have a simple but effective poem.

② A psychologist called "Rorsharch" invented a test based on similar ink blots. You could make your own by simply making a crease in the centre of a piece of paper, placing a small amount of ink near the crease on one side and folding it over so that the ink smudges. Carefully unfold the paper and leave it to dry.

③ Psychologists have used such tests to judge people's personalities. They consider such things as whether the person responds to the whole ink blot or just part of it, what the person sees in the ink blot, whether the person sees something moving or still. Do different people in the class see different things in the ink blots? One person might see butterflies, flowers, a sunset - whereas someone else might see a dark tunnel, a monster, an explosion.

Poets and other writers help us to see things in different and imaginative ways.

A Walk At Night

I thought I saw a twisted hand which pointed in
the air,
I looked again and saw a tree with branches gnarled
and bare.
I thought I saw a giant footprint stamped across
the lawn,
It was a shadow of a hedge with edges badly torn.
I thought I saw a row of drumsticks standing in
the ground,
It was a row of dandelions with seed pods strewn
around.
I thought I saw a hooded figure calling me to follow,
It was a statue of a man inside a leafy hollow.
I ran indoors and thought I saw a face look wild
with fright
I looked again and saw I had a mirror in my sight.

Chris Evans

THROUGH MY MAGNIFYING GLASS

The spider and the web are transformed,
A lurking monster waits to kill
In a shimmering web;
Expanse of lethal attraction.

(4) Write a list of everyday objects which you
might see at night and then describe what you
think they might remind you of if you let your
imagination work on them. What might the
following look like in the dark: a telephone box,
a street lamp, cats' eyes in the road, a belisha
beacon?

(5) Have you ever looked into a fire and thought
you saw objects and faces in the flames?
Have you ever seen faces in the branches of
trees? Choose one of the following phrases
for the start of a paragraph of about four
sentences which describes what you have
seen. " *I stared into the flames of the fire and
saw...*", "*I looked up at the sky and saw...*",
"*I looked at the shadows of the trees cast by
the moon on my bedroom wall and saw...*".

Now try . . . . . .

6 Try writing a poem of your
own called "Through my
Magnifying Glass".

7 Write a story which
describes how it felt to be in
the world described by your
poem and illustrate it.

Geography Lesson

With Highland hair and arms of Wales
Reaching for Ireland, England trails
A lonely distance behind Europe
Trying impossibly to cheer up:
A sloppy nurse who hopes that maybe
No one will see she's dropped her baby
Splash into the Irish Sea
While bouncing on her knee.

With hips of Norfolk and Kent,
Her posture's more than strangely bent.
Yorkshire gives backache with its Ridings.
The Midlands, full of railway sidings,
She blames for burps of indigestion.
Her Birmingham has got congestion.
Her Derbyshire is full of holes.
London's asleep at the controls
And her subconscious shifts the worry
Out to Middlesex and Surrey.

Yet Devon's a comfortable shoe
From which old Cornwall's toes peep
through.
On Lleyn, sedately, Anglesey
Is balanced like a cup of tea,
While clucking in her tea-time mirth
Her mouth's the open Solway Firth
Ready to swallow if she can
The little cake of the Isle of Man.

Even asleep she falls apart:
Dreams of the Orkneys make her start
And stitches of the Isle of Wight
Drop off from Hampshire in the night.
With bits of knitting in the Channel,
Most of East Anglia wrapped in flannel
And snores exhaling from Argyll,
The dear old lady makes you smile:
What can you do with such a creature
To whom each country lends a feature?
She'll still be there when I am gone
Through all your lives she'll shamble on,
Grubby, forgetful, laughing, hatless -
The silliest country in the atlas.

John Fuller

(1) ☆ The poet who wrote *Geography Lesson* has found a very imaginative way of using the British Isles. From the information given in the poem and from the drawing, mark all the places the poet mentions on a map of the British Isles.

In the following passage Emma has just discovered that her colour-blindness has been cured.

She clenched her fists, remaining very still; but her heart raced as she thought, "It's happened! It's happened! Oh God! Thank you! It's happened!" And yet was it possible? Could such a thing happen?

Emma opened her right eye just a fraction, so that she could see between her eyelashes, and it was true. There was the green of grass, sown with buttercups and dandelions like brass buttons, and the white petals and yellow centres of daisies.

A sudden chill of fear struck her and she closed her eyes again. This was very, very dangerous. She had read descriptions of colour in books, and people had told her what things look like in colour, but none of them conveyed to her even the tiniest fraction of what she had already seen was the most miraculous and beautiful thing in the whole world, the infinitely varied glory of colour. There was not one green, but tens of thousands of different shades of green; and when they said grass was green, it was also yellow and brown and nearly black in places, and in others nearly white.

Perhaps people who had seen colour all their lives had never noticed that, or had just grown lazy about looking, calling grass green because it was more green than it was any other colour. And then she would be tempted to tell them that they had never really looked at colour, and they would say, "How do you know?" They would laugh and say, "You're colour-blind and yet you pretend to know." And then she would be tempted to say what had happened.

She opened her eyes again as she heard a crack and a burst of applause. . The red ball bounded towards her across the grass, a white-clad, sweating shiny-black-haired man pounding behind it. He flung his arms up as it crossed the boundary. The inside of the arm was pink and smooth, the outside covered with golden hairs, the skin red-brown underneath. He flung the ball to the bowler as the batsmen walked back to their wickets.

The sky was not one but a dozen shades of blue varying in depth. Where there was thick woolly cloud, the blue of the sky around was darker than at the edges of thin feathery clouds. That means, Emma thought, a colour is not its colour all by itself, but what it's next to changes it. She saw that the sun on the top of the roof of the cottage silhouetted against the sky made a line of light green between the red roof and the grey of the cloud beyond ....

Then she remembered that Druce the chemist had a weighing-machine in the entrance to his shop, and in the centre of its face she thought there was a mirror. Druce's was in the middle of the village, but she ran there and reached it out of breath. The moment she saw that there was a mirror, she stopped running.

She walked slowly up to it, approaching it from the side. Then gingerly she peered round at her reflection.

Her heart sank.

Now try . . . . . .

2 How do you think the passage continues? Write what you imagine the next paragraph might have been.

3 Imagine that you are looking at something through Emma's eyes. In other words you have seen it in shades of grey until this moment and now you see it in colour for the first time. Because of this you take more notice of the colours than people who have not been colour-blind. The brown table top may have shades of different colours, streaks of black. What would be your reaction to other objects - a jacket, a poster on the wall, a pencil case? Write a paragraph describing the colours you see as exactly as you can.

4 Go through the passage and identify all the different colours Emma notices and say what it is she is looking at.

5 Write an account of someone who has either just been cured of colour-blindness or has just regained their sight after being blind. Imagine how they might feel but try to SHOW that in your writing rather than TELL the reader. Rather than write, *"She was delighted..."*, describe what it is she can now see which she could not before. You could begin *"For the first time....."*

10.1 UFOs.

This unit is about UFOs (unidentified flying objects). In it you will find emphasis on distinguishing fact from fiction, looking at things in different ways and the use of prepositions.

> **DO YOU THINK WE ARE BEING VISITED BY LIFE FORMS FROM OTHER PLANETS?**

ILLUSIONS AND FRAUDS

Lightning or aliens?

A flock of geese at night or UFOs?

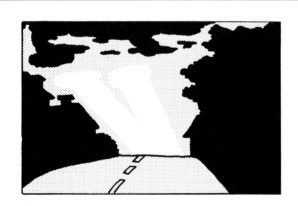

Car lights over the brow of a hill or an alien craft?

A fake photograph or a craft from Mars?

1 Sometimes people think they have seen a UFO and it turns out that there is a perfectly ordinary explanation. Other reports of UFOs have simply been fakes. Choose two of the pictures above and write to "Skywatchers", a society which investigates UFO sightings, saying exactly what you saw and where you were. Your job is to convince them that your sighting is worth investigating.

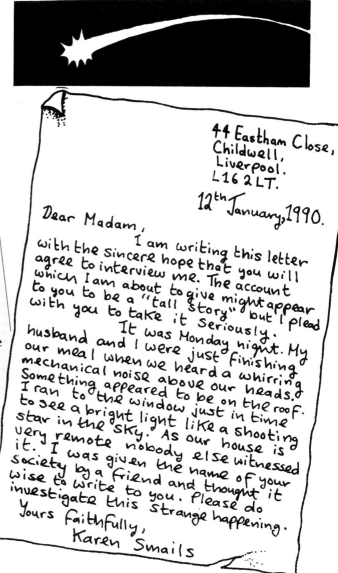

74 Queens Park Court,
London.
W10 4PQ

2 December 1989

Dear Sir,
I would very much like to join your association. Recently I witnessed a strange sight which I have since been unable to explain. While walking in the countryside on a clear evening I was looking into the evening sky and to my astonishment I spotted a strange light in the sky. The light was white and about the size of a small ball. It travelled across the sky at a fantastic speed, stopped then disappeared. I then started to scan the sky seriously and spotted another seven similar lights. Some of the lights appeared at the same time and travelled in the same direction. I am convinced that these were spaceships from another planet. If you accepted me as a member of your society I would be able to supply more information.

Yours faithfully,

Gareth O'Brien.

44 Eastham Close,
Childwell,
Liverpool.
L16 2LT.
12th January, 1990.

Dear Madam,
I am writing this letter with the sincere hope that you will agree to interview me. The account which I am about to give might appear to you to be a "tall story" but I plead with you to take it seriously.
It was Monday night. My husband and I were just finishing our meal when we heard a whirring mechanical noise above our heads. Something appeared to be on the roof. I ran to the window just in time to see a bright light like a shooting star in the sky. As our house is very remote nobody else witnessed it. I was given the name of your society by a friend and thought it wise to write to you. Please do investigate this strange happening.
Yours faithfully,
Karen Smails

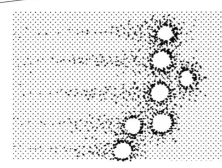

Now try . . . . . .

2 Write a report to Skywatchers' committee giving your opinion about each letter saying whether you think it is genuine. Choose one letter which you think merits further investigation and give your reasons.

3 Imagine that a member of Skywatchers interviews the author of one of the above letters. In pairs conduct the interview.

4 In groups hold a meeting of the Skywatchers committee to discuss the letters and the results of the interviews. It is the group's job to make a final decision as to which case merits further investigation.

5 Having chosen which letter to investigate, you now have to prepare a plan of how to go about the investigation. Write down that plan. You might need to interview more people, take photographs, conduct a search of the area, carry out experiments to see if the evidence could have been faked, or conduct research to see if there could be a simple explanation for what was seen. Try to find out if there have been any UFO sightings in your area. The local library might be able to help, and so might the local newspaper.

UFO DEATH RIDDLE

The unexplained death of a man is at the centre of one of the most amazing UFO mystery stories yet.

The body of Joseph Cotterell was found in a field, 200 yards behind his house where he lived on his own on the outskirts of Northampton. Strange, unexplained burn marks covered his body and experts believe that he could have died of fright. A policewoman who was called to the scene reported sighting what looked like a flying saucer overhead only hours before.

Extensive enquiries ordered by the coroner have failed to suggest any normal reason for Mr. Cotterell's death. The coroner told us that this was the most mysterious death he had investigated in his entire career. Mr. Cotterell was said to be a quiet man who kept himself to himself. Neighbours reported that they had never known him to set foot inside

the field where he was found, and they could think of no reason why he should suddenly do so.

The burns covering his body appear to have been caused by a corrosive substance which penetrated his clothes but which, so far, experts have failed to identify.

The police officer in charge of the investigation, Inspector Bainbridge, told us, "We have absolutely nothing to go on, apart from the body and a mysterious, circular burnt patch of ground in the field. At this stage we discount nothing but, as policemen, we have to rely on facts. It is true that some reports have come in about a UFO sighting in the area at about the time of death, but these are unconfirmed."

Another policeman, also involved in the investigation but who wished to remain anonymous, told us, "Experts have so far failed to identify the corrosive substance and the only explanation that fits the facts is that a UFO

was involved. I cannot speculate about this, but while I have been on this case I have looked into other reported UFO sightings. There are thousands of such reports, coming from almost every country in the world and going back in time through the ages. It is difficult to believe that they are all a result of human error. I am inclined to think that there may be some truth in the UFO theory."

---

① This article appeared on the inside of the newspaper but you as editor had the job of writing a summary of no more than sixty words and no fewer than fifty to fill a space on the front page. The short paragraph will end with the sentence "Full story inside".

② What evidence is there in the article which suggests that the event was caused by a UFO?

③ What evidence is there to suggest that such an explanation is unlikely?

④ Can you suggest a "normal" explanation for what happened? It needs to fit the facts, but exclude any possibility of a UFO.

⑤ Why do you think the last policeman quoted wished to remain anonymous?

⑥ Write your own newspaper headline and article based on a strange encounter with a UFO.
 You may illustrate it if you wish.

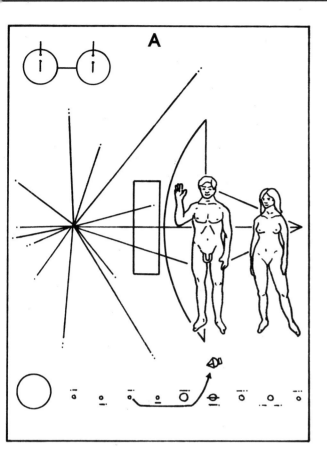

A

This plaque was attached to Pioneer 10, the first spacecraft to leave the solar system. The plaque indicates the craft's origin in case it is found by other beings.

7 In pairs, try to work out the significance of every item in the picture A. Write down your conclusions in note form.

8 Skywatchers have been asked to prepare a statement of 100 words which will be sent to distant star constellations by radio signal in the hope that it will be received and understood by other life forms. Write the statement you would send in no more than 100 words.

9 What are your views on UFOs and the likelihood of there being life on other planets? Write what you think in three or four paragraphs.

Are there living creatures anywhere else in the universe? There are millions of stars in the universe and many of them are likely to have planets orbiting them. It is not so far-fetched to think that there may be life on another planet somewhere. It is a very difficult question, however, when we ask whether we will ever make contact with life on another planet.

We are fairly certain that there is no intelligent life on planets which are quite near to us. As for other planets the difficulty comes in the huge distances which would have to be covered in order to find out. The Pioneer 10 was launched in 1972. It is now far out of our solar system, but it has still not travelled far compared with the huge distances in space. In 1977 Voyager 2 was launched by the USA. Both spacecraft may travel through the universe for millions of years and may be seen some day by the inhabitants of a planet.

Many astronomers listen for radio messages from distant planets. Similarly we send radio signals into space. One such message was sent out in 1974 to a group of stars in the constellation Hercules. However, the message will take 24,000 years to get there.

Now try . . . . . .

10 Imagine that a space ship has been visiting earth from another planet. The visitors have been observing us for some time. They send back a report to their planet on what they have observed about human beings and their way of life. Write the report.

If you look at the diagrams below you will be able to work out how this photograph was faked.

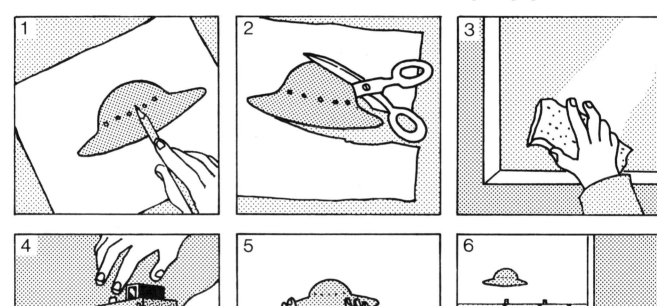

(2) Can you think of other ways of faking a UFO picture? Make your own fake UFO photographs. Display them on the wall, accompanied by appropriate newspaper articles.

 REMINDER - Prepositions.

Ellie was waiting *with* Arif *for* Spike. She gave the photograph *to* Arif. He was surprised to find the outline *of* a UFO *in* the picture. All three walked *by* the newsagent's shop *at* the corner and *along* Canal Street *towards* the police station.

All the words in italics are PREPOSITIONS. A preposition joins words or parts of a sentence together, most often showing how the two parts are related in space and time. It is the most difficult part of speech to recognise. It is always placed before the word or words to which it is referring, e.g. The UFO is *in* the picture.

Do not confuse a PREPOSITION with a CONJUNCTION. A preposition shows how words are related; a conjunction just links words or collections of words, e.g. The alien *and* his friends climbed out of the spacecraft.

(3) Supply prepositions to fill in the spaces in the following passage.

I looked..... the sky. "Is there life..... other planets," I wondered. The nearest star is millions of miles away so that many stars we see have actually disappeared. The reason is that although light travels .... space extremely fast, the distances are so great that it takes a long time for the light to reach us.
"Could I travel faster than the speed of light?" I thought.
If I could travel...... the other side of the room I would be able to see myself. If I see stars...... the sky which disappeared years ago, what would I see if I travelled...... space faster than light? I would see myself as a baby. If I went faster I would be able to see Roman Britain.
I started to get a headache. I went ..... the house and watched the television.

(4) Just imagine you are in a strange alien craft and you enter a room which is completely dark. You have to cross the room - in the dark - and go out through another opening opposite. Describe your journey in detail.

Remember, you cannot see anything. Before you start to write, decide what sort of room it is - control room, engine room, sleeping quarters or whatever - and then decide how to cross to the other side. You will feel very carefully so as not to crash into anything. But you won't necessarily know what it is you are feeling, so you will need to describe what it feels like. Begin:

"I opened the door and stepped cautiously into the completely dark room."

(5) When you have finished count how many prepositions you have used.

In this unit you will be using language in a variety of imaginative ways and thinking about how language can be used to achieve different effects.

THEY HAVE YARNS OF THE YOUNG WOMAN WHO TURNED OLD IF YOU STARED AT HER FOR A LONG TIME.

Look carefully at the picture. Is it a picture of a young woman looking away or an old woman with a large nose?

They have yarns

They have yarns
Of a skyscraper so tall they had to put hinges
On the two storeys so as to let the moon go by.
Of one corn crop in Missouri when the roots
Went so deep and drew off so much water
The Mississippi river bed that year was dry.
Of pancakes so thin they had only one side.
Of "a fog so thick we shingled the barn and six feet
out onto the fog".
Of Pecos Pete straddling a cyclone in Texas and
riding it to the west-coast where it rained out
under him.
Of the man who drove a swarm of bees across the
Rocky Mountains and the desert and didn't
lose a bee.
Of a mountain railroad curve where the engineer
in his cab can touch the caboose and spit in the
conductor's eye.
Of the boy who climbed a cornstalk growing so
fast he would have starved to death if they hadn't
shot biscuits up to him.
Of the old man's whiskers: "When the wind
was with him his whiskers arrived a day before
he did."
Of the hen laying a square egg and cackling
"Ouch!" and of hens laying eggs with the dates
printed on them.
Of the ship's captain's shadow: it froze to the deck
one cold winter night.
Of mutineers on that same ship put to chipping rust with rubber hammers.
Of the sheep counter who was fast and accurate: "I just count their feet and divide by four."
Of the man so tall he must climb a ladder to shave himself.
Of the runt so teeny-weeny it takes two men and a boy to see him.
Of mosquitoes: one can kill a dog, two of them a man.

Carl Sandburg

THE WHOPPER

ALIENS VISIT EARTH !

Creatures from an alien planet landed yesterday in the South of England. They were first spotted by a farmer who said he found them trying to make conversation with his horse. They did not seem the least bit frightened and are now on their way to London.

POP STAR BECOMES PRIME MINISTER! FULL STORY INSIDE

(1) Choose the three yarns you like best.

(2) Choose one of the yarns and present it in the form of a magazine article. Treat it
☆ seriously - the more seriously you treat it the more absurd and amusing it will be. Include drawings and quotations from people.

(3) Try to invent some yarns of your own. Use a sentence for each yarn starting the sentence with the words *"They have yarns ..."*. Remember to start the sentence with a capital letter and end with a full stop.

Here are some sentences for you to complete.

They have yarns of the lion whose mouth was so big ...
They have yarns of the teacher who shouted so loud ...
They have yarns of the boy who had a tongue so long ...
They have yarns of the star which shone so bright ..

Now try to make up four sentences of your own.
Have you written a poem?

(4) Make a list of slang words (either ones currently used or ones which are no longer used) for the following:
- Money - dosh, dough, bread, etc.
- Excellent - brill, fab, ace, etc.
- Fashionable - cool, hip, groovy, etc.
- Stupid person - dimwit, nit, etc.

(5) Can you think of any other groups of slang words all meaning the same thing?

(6) There are times when it is not really suitable to use slang, e.g. a vicar giving a sermon, a judge in court, meeting the queen, a Head taking assembly, reading the news.
Choose a situation in which slang would not be appropriate and write either a conversation in which one person is using slang, or a speech using slang.

SLANG is a use of language which is informal. There are a number of slang words for lies such as "whoppers" or "porkies". In groups, your job is to produce a newspaper which contains nothing but lies. So that people will know that you are **not** really trying to deceive them and that it is just in fun, call your newspaper something which means "lies" or "the lie".

e.g. **THE WHOPPER** ☆

Your paper can be about politicians, people in the class, the school, pop stars or whatever. Have fun - make it as unlikely as you want!

Slang terms go in and out of fashion fairly quickly. Some words which were used a few years ago are no longer used.

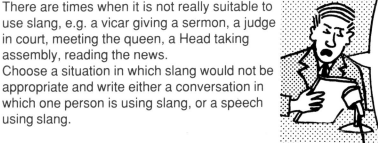

EVENING ALL . HERE ARE THE NEWS HEADLINES . A PILE OF DOSH WAS HALF-INCHED FROM THE BANK OF ENGLAND TODAY. ONE OLD GEEZER GOT COSHED ON HIS BONCE AND IS IN HOSPITAL. HE TOOK A RIGHT PASTING . . . .

11.2 Language Matters.

Different situations demand different types of language for different audiences. Language is a powerful tool - if you can use it appropriately. Consider the following two exchanges. The facts are the same in both cases and you may recognise them. The excuse might not work in either case, but which one do you think would be more likely to succeed?

First Exchange

Teacher: Have you done your homework?
Pupil: Nah - couldn't be bothered, like. Me and me mate was larking around in me dad's shop. He kicked us out in the end 'n' by then we was right shattered so we 'ad some chips, watched telly and kipped down.

Second Exchange

Teacher: Have you done your homework?
Pupil: Sorry, Miss, but I had to help with my friend in my dad's shop last night. By the time he didn't need us any more it was so late there was only time to have supper and then go to bed.

(1) Consider the following situations:

(a) You forgot to see a teacher, and the teacher later accosts you and asks for an explanation.

(b) You borrow a book from the school or local library and without thinking you walk out with it, not stopping to have it issued to you. The librarian catches up with you outside.

(c) The owner of an apple tree catches you eating his or her apples. They are windfalls and you assumed no-one would mind.

You can try this out in pairs, or with a teacher taking one part, or with any visitors to the school who are willing to join in. The last might be more effective because they would be strangers to you. Take any of the situations and role play in pairs. Take it in turns to play the opposing roles. Discuss how you felt, what happened and why the accused has to try to talk his or her way out of the situation, using language as effectively as possible.

WORDS WORDS WORDS WORDS WORDS

Have you ever been in the sort of situation that Linda finds herself in below?

Linda looked at her watch. It was only ten minutes past two which meant that there were still three hours of the flight to go. Getting to the airport had been fun and so had take-off even though her ears had popped, but now she was beginning to get bored. She opened her small rucksack and looked at the contents: a pack of cards, three comics, a couple of books, a note-pad and two electronic games. She didn't feel like doing any of those. It was going to be a long wait. At that moment the air steward came down the isle and handed her a booklet and a pencil. "That should keep you busy," he said. Linda looked at the title - it simply said "WORDS". She turned to the first page and got to work ... Before she knew it, the plane was ready to land.

(2) Your job is to create the booklet which keeps Linda busy. It is built around language games, puzzles, jokes and riddles.
☆ Here are some suggestions for you to include: crazy book-titles, puns and ambiguities, crosswords, word-searches, anagrams, limericks. You may think of other ideas as well, and the rest of this unit might give you some suggestions.
On the next page you will find some ideas that you might use. You might find it a good idea to keep the whole booklet to one theme, e.g. sport, pop stars, or whatever.

CRAZY BOOK TITLES

"Sinking Ship" by Mandy Lifeboat
"Off the Cliff" by Eileen Dover.

PUNS AND AMBIGUITIES

You make puns with words that have the same sound but different meanings. Many jokes rely on puns. They are often jokes which make you want to groan.
"Where do you take a sick horse?" "Horsepital."

Many things we say in English have two possible meanings - they are ambiguous. We often don't realise this at the time, like the teacher who said, "Now children, watch the blackboard while I go through it". "Doctor, Doctor" jokes rely on ambiguity. Advertisements often play with double meanings, too. The following is an advertisement for a particular kind of trifle. OURS IS A TRIFLE MORE DELICIOUS.

Headlines in newspapers, too, are sometimes ambiguous, not always on purpose, as in: - BOY SUSPENDED BY HEAD.

ANAGRAMS

These are words made by rearranging the letters of other words, e.g. FORMER CHEAT (Form teacher)

LIMERICKS

You should recognise these as silly poems of five lines which always rhyme in the same way. Work out the pattern of rhyme.

> There was a young lady from Crete,
> Who had two spectacular feet.
> When she hopped on a bus
> There was no room for us,
> Her feet took up every spare seat.

As well as having a fixed rhyme scheme, limericks have a fixed rhythm. You can hear it when you read one out, and you can see it if you use / to represent a syllable you stress and **u** to represent a weaker or unstressed syllable. The pattern should be:

u/uu/uu/
u/uu/uu/
uu/uu/
uu/uu/
u/uu/uu/

When you write a limerick of your own, write it out in rough first. Then read it out loud. Try marking the stressed and unstressed syllables with a pencil.

SPOONERISMS

Spoonerisms are named after a certain Rev. W.A. Spooner who taught at Oxford University in the nineteenth century. He is reputed to have told an unsatisfactory student: - "You have tasted two worms. You have hissed all my mystery lectures and you will leave by the first town drain." The student's reply is not recorded.

There are three spoonerisms in that speech. A spoonerism occurs when the first letter or letters of two words change place, creating new, surprising effects!

Good spoonerisms make sense - however weirdly.

You are a boiled sprat!
I love you so much I'm going to give you a hair bug!
Are there any bare spooks in here?
I buy and sell shocks and stares.

(1) Collect and make up your own spoonerisms. Try talking to each other in pairs, deliberately making spoonerisms. Most won't be much good, but every now and then you will find one that is. Make a note of the good ones and share them with the class later.

YOU BOILED SPRAT!

WOULD YOU PLEASE HUSH MY BRAT! ITS ROARING WITH PAIN

His eyes are as shiny as the creases in my trousers!

SIMILES

Similes are created when we compare one thing with another by saying it is **LIKE** something else. It is usually like it in only one respect.

We use expressions like "dead as a doornail" or "flat as a pancake" without thinking. These similes have been used so often they have lost their impact. Have you ever seen a live doornail!

But new similes, that no-one has heard before, can be very effective.

(A) He consumes food like a pig.
(B) He consumes food like a waste disposal unit.
Which one do you think is the better?

(2) Invent six new similes that are lively and entertaining.

HOMOPHONES

"Which hour, Witch?"
"Watch your watch."
"Where will you wear that jacket?"
"Oh dear! Dear deer, dear," said a man to his wife when he saw the price of a piece of venison.

Homophones are words that sound the same but are spelt differently

③ How many homophones can you find? A dictionary might help you. Select FIVE sounds and make up five sentences which look all right on paper but are VERY confusing when you read them out loud. For some of the sounds you might find more than two words.

"Faith can move mountains. She's a very big girl!"

"What is the wettest animal?"
"A reindeer!"

"May I join you?"
"Why, am I coming apart?"

"WHAT WEARS A COAT ALL WINTER, AND PANTS ALL SUMMER?"
"A DOG!"

Foolish Question

Where can a man buy a cap for his knee?
Or a key for the lock of his hair?
And can his eyes be called a school?
I would think - there are pupils there.
What jewels are found in the crown of his head,
And who walks on the bridge of his nose?
Can he use, in building the roof of his mouth,
The nails on the ends of his toes?
Can the crook of his elbow be sent to jail -
If it can, well, then what did it do?
And how does he sharpen his shoulder blades?
I'll be hanged if I know - do you?
Can he sit in the shade of the palm of his hand,
And beat time with the drum of his ear?
Can the calf of his leg eat the corn on his toe?
There's something pretty strange around here!

American Folk Rhyme
Adapted by William Cole

FOOLISH QUESTIONS

If it's on the tip of your tongue, can you taste it? If you take all the time in the world, will there be any left for me?

English is a strange language!

Can you think of more questions which draw your attention to literal meanings of common sayings like those above?
Some expressions you might use are: laughing your head off; falling head over heels in love; raising the roof.
Think up more of your own and make up questions which treat them literally.

④ Write down your questions using a line for each. Have you written a poem?

Tha cannot have it every road ah bet that dogs a rare ratter. Tha cannot guarantee em tha knows...

Uncle Time is a de, de man.... All year long 'im wash 'im foot in de sea...

Och! I hae me doots. I'll mak it guid, but nae promises...

Well you see this bloke didn know nuffin did he. I asked im and he says to me...

You will be aware that people speak differently. People from different countries speak different languages.

Some people speak the same language but have different accents - they pronounce words differently.

Other people speak different dialects - they use different words, e.g. in the North East children are called "bairns". Very often people from different areas have different accents and use dialect words.

Salut!

Comment va ta famille? Tout va bien chez nous.

— Hei! mitä kuuluu? Perheeni vai hyvin.

1 In pairs take it in turns to read the extracts in the picture aloud. Can you guess where the speaker comes from in each case?

2 Write a short speech (weather forecast, announcement at assembly, news flash, or an idea of your own) EITHER in your local dialect OR in one of the dialects in the picture. Notice the way the spelling shows how to pronounce the words.

3 ☆ Look at a map of the British Isles and find the places where the four accents illustrated are spoken. Can you identify any other regions with strong accents?

4 In groups of five or six find out the following information:
How many languages are spoken in the group, either by members of the groups or by families.
How many accents do the members of your group have?
How many accents can you think of among the staff of your school?
Can you think of any dialect words used in your area? List as many as you can.
Can the members of your group mimic any accents?
Can you identify the languages below? They are all saying much the same thing: - "Hello. How is your family? We are all very well."

我們大家都很好。
喂！你們好嗎？

Now try . . . . . .

5 ☆ Tape as many accents and foreign languages as you can and bring them into school to share with the class. Find out what you can about the place where the accents come from.

The following are samples of English writing through the ages. You can probably understand most of what they say. Two of the passages are about the same incident from different versions of the Bible, more than 350 years apart. Which version do you prefer and why?

Upon the cop right of his nose he hade
A werte, and theron stood a toft of herys,
Teed as the brustles of a sowes erys;
His nosethirles blake were and wyde.
A swerd bokeler bar be by his syde.

"Mr Squeers," said the waiter, looking in at this juncture, "Here's a gentleman asking for you at the bar."
"Show the gentleman in Richard," replied Mr. Squeers, in a soft voice. "Put your handkerchief in your pocket, you little scoundrel, or I'll murder you when the gentleman goes." The schoolmaster had scarcely uttered these words in a fierce whisper, when the stranger entered. Affecting not to see him, Mr. Squeers feigned to be intent upon mending a pen, and offering benevolent advice to his youthful pupil.

Goliath started walking towards David again, and David ran quickly towards the Philistine battle line to fight him. He put his hand into his bag and took out a stone, which he slung at Goliath. It hit him on the forehead and broke his skull, and Goliath fell face downwards on the ground. And so, without a sword, David defeated and killed Goliath with a catapult and a stone!
He ran to him, stood over him, took Goliath's sword out of its sheath, and cut off his head and killed him. When the Philistines saw that their hero was dead, they ran away!

And it came to pass, when the Philistine arose, and came and drew nigh to meet David, that David hasted, and ran toward the army to meet the Philistine. And David put his hand in his bag, and took thence a stone, and slang it, and smote the Philistine in his forehead, that the stone sunk into his forehead; and fell upon his face to the earth.
So David prevailed over the Philistine with a sling and with a stone, and smote the Philistine, and slew him; but there was no sword in the hand of David. Therefore David ran, and stood upon the Philistine, and took his sword, and drew it out of the sheath thereof, and slew him, and cut off his head therewith. And when the Philistine saw their champion was dead, they fled!

6   The first passage, by Chaucer, was written about six hundred years ago. Many of the words used then are no longer used today, and some have changed greatly.
"Nosethirles" is still in use, but the spelling and pronunciation has changed. It is now "nostrils".

Can you think of words we have now which they did not have in Chaucer's time? To start with, think of things which were not invented then.

7   New words are being invented all the time. Try inventing words for the following: hair at the end of someone's nose; a brand new make of car; nail clippings.

In this unit you will be encouraged to read widely and think about - and enjoy - what you read.

Here are the front covers of some novels with the description given on the back of the book.

Rukshana Smith

Rainbows of the Gutter   £3.95

"A young black artist looks at his life from the time he was 10, and at what the reality of being black in Britain has done to his dream of a multi-ethnic society where races and cultures blend, neither retreating from, nor attacking each other.....provocative, thoughtful (earnest indeed), and sometimes painful."
The Guardian.

128pp	*198x126*	*(1983)*
Second impression		*ISBN 0 370 30526 4*

(1) If you were choosing one of these books to read which one would it be and why? (If you have read any already, leave them out of your choice.)

(2) What do you think might happen in the book you have chosen, judging by the information you are given on the cover?

(3) Look at each description and say whether the book seems to be aimed at boys, girls or both boys and girls.

(4) Write a paragraph called "My Reading Tastes" and describe the sort of reading you enjoy. Include comics, magazines, fiction, non-fiction, books at school, etc. Have your tastes changed over the years? You could also include information about when and where you read.

Sumitra's Story   £3.95

A semi-documentary account of the problems faced by a young Ugandan Asian growing up in Britain. Finding herself torn between her restrictive Hindu up-bringing and the more liberal Western attitudes that surround her at school and at work, Sumitra struggles to define her own identity, her own values. **Winner of the first Garavi Gujarat Award for Racial Harmony, 1982.**

160pp	*198x126*	*(1982)*
Third Impression		*ISBN 0370 30466 7*

WHEN YOU READ A NOVEL OR STORY DO YOU

- picture the places you read about in your mind?
- compare characters to people in real life?
- try to predict what will happen in the story?
- imagine what it would be like to be one of the characters?

Now try ......

5 Describe in four easy stages how you go about looking up a book in the library.

6 Make a class booklet of recommended reading. This could include a non-fiction as well as a fiction section. If each member of the class recommends two or three titles you will have quite a long list. Remember to include the author, title and publisher.

Read the following story by Jan Mark, called *"The Choice is Yours"*, pausing to think every now and then about what you are reading. Do not pause for too long as this will spoil the flow of the story, but make sure you respond to all the questions.

Have you ever had to make up your mind and choose between two events, both of which you wanted to attend?

The Music Room was on one side of the quadrangle and the Changing Room faced it on the other. They were linked by a corridor that made up the third side, and the fourth was the view across the playing-fields. In the Music Room Miss Helen Francis sat at the piano, head bent over the keyboard as her finger tittuped from note to note, and swaying back and forth like a snake charming itself. At the top of the Changing Room steps Miss Marion Taylor stood, sportively poised with one hand on the doorknob and a whistle dangling on a string from the other; quivering with eagerness to be out on the field and inhaling fresh air. They could see each other. Brenda, standing in the doorway of the Music Room, could see them both.

> **Can you tell from the opening paragraph what choice Brenda will be forced to make?**

"Well, come on, child," said Miss Francis. "Don't haver. If you must haver, don't do it in the doorway. Other people are trying to come in."

Brenda moved to one side to make way for other people, members of the choir who would normally have shoved her out of the way and pushed past. Here they shed their school manners in the corridor and queued in attitudes of excruciated patience. Miss Helen Francis favoured the noiseless approach. Across the quadrangle the Under-Thirteen Hockey XI roistered, and Miss Marion Taylor failed to intervene. Miss Francis observed all this with misty disapproval and looked away again.

"Brenda dear, are you coming in, or going out, or putting down roots?"

The rest of the choir was by now seated; first sopranos on the right, second sopranos on the left, thirds across one end and Miss Humphry, who was billed as an alto but sang tenor, at the other. They all sat up straight, as trained by Miss Francis, and looked curiously at Brenda who should have been seated too, among the first sopranos. Her empty chair was in the front row, with the music stacked on it, all ready. Miss Francis cocked her head to one side like a budgerigar that sees a millet spray in the offing.

"Have you a message for us dear? From above?" She meant the headmistress, but by her tone it could have been God and his angels.

"No, Miss Francis."

"From beyond?"

"Miss Francis, can I ask -?"

"You may ask, Brenda. Whether or not you can is beyond my powers of divination."

Brenda saw that the time for havering was at an end.

"Please Miss Francis, may I be excused from choir?"

The budgie instantly turned into a marabou stork.

"Excused, Brenda? Do you have a pain?"

"There's a hockey practice, Miss Francis."

"I am aware of that." Miss Francis cast a look, over her shoulder and across the quadrangle, that should have turned Miss Taylor to stone, and the Under-Thirteen XI with her. "How does it concern you, Brenda? How does it concern me?"

The Choice is Yours.

What impression are you starting to get of
Miss Francis? Do you know any people like
her? Would you like to have her as a teacher?

"I'm in the team, Miss Francis, and there's a match
on Saturday," said Brenda.

"But, my dear," Miss Francis smiled at her with
surpassing sweetness. "I think my mind must be
going." She lifted limp fingers from the keyboard
and touched them on her forehead as if to arrest the
absconding mind. "Hockey practices are on Tuesdays
and Fridays. Choir practices are on Mondays and
Thursdays. It was ever thus. Today is Thursday.
Everyone else thinks it's Thursday, otherwise they
wouldn't be here." She swept out a spare arm that
encompassed the waiting choir and asked helplessly,
"It is Thursday, isn't it? You all think it's Thursday?
It's not just me having a little brainstorm?"

The choir tittered, sotto voce, to assure Miss Francis
that it was indeed Thursday, and to express its mass
contempt for anyone who was fool enough to get
caught in the cross-fire between Miss Francis and
Miss Taylor.

"It's a match against the High School, Miss Francis.
Miss Taylor called a special practice," said Brenda,
hoping that her mention of the High School might
save her, for if Miss Francis loathed anyone more
than she loathed Miss Taylor, it was the music
mistress at the High School. If the match had been
against the High School choir, it might have been a
different matter, and Miss Francis might have been
out on the side-lines chanting with the rest of them:

"Two - four - six - eight, who - do - we - hate?"

Miss Francis, however, was not to be deflected.

"You know that I do not allow any absence from
choir without a very good reason. Now, will you sit
down, please?" She turned gaily to face the room. "I
think we'll begin with Schubert."

"Please. May I go and tell Miss Taylor that I can't
come?"

Miss Francis sighed a sigh that turned a page on
the music stand.

"Two minutes, Brenda. We'll wait," she said
venomously, and set the metronome ticking on the
piano so that they might all count the two minutes,
second by second.

Miss Taylor still stood upon the steps of the
Changing Room. While they were all counting, they
could turn round and watch Brenda tell Miss Taylor
that she was not allowed to attend hockey practice.
Tock.

Tock.
Tock.

Brenda closed the door on the ticking and began
to run. She would have to run to be there and back
in two minutes, and running in the corridors was
forbidden.

Miss Taylor had legs like bath loofahs stuffed into
long, hairy grey socks, that were held up by tourniquets
of narrow elastic. When she put on her stockings
after school and mounted her bicycle to pedal
strenuously home up East Hill, you could still see
the twin red marks, like the rubber seals on Kilner
jars. The loofahs were the first things that Brenda
saw as she mounted the steps, and the grey socks
bristled with impatience.

What do you think will happen when Brenda
gets to Miss Taylor?

"Practice begins at twelve fifty," said Miss Taylor.
"I suppose you were thinking of joining us?"

Brenda began to cringe all over again.

"Please, Miss Taylor, Miss Francis says I can't
come."

"Does she? And what's it got to do with Miss
Francis? Are you in detention?"

"No, Miss Taylor. I'm in choir."

"You may only be the goalkeeper, Brenda, but we
still expect you to turn out for practices. You'll have

to explain to Miss Francis that she must manage without you for once. I don't imagine that the choir will collapse if you're missing."

"No, Miss Taylor."

"Go on then, at the double. We'll wait."

Brenda ran down the steps, aware of the Music Room windows, but not looking at them, and back into the corridor. Halfway along it she was halted by a shout from behind.

"What do you think you're doing?"

Brenda turned and saw the Head Girl, Gill Rogers, who was also the school hockey captain and had the sense not to try and sing as well.

"Running, Gill. Sorry, Gill."

"Running's forbidden. You know that. Go back and walk."

"Miss Taylor told me to run."

"It's no good trying to blame Miss Taylor; I'm sure she didn't tell you to run."

"She said at the double," said Brenda.

"That's not the same thing at all. Go back and walk."

Brenda went back and walked.

"Two minutes and fifteen seconds," said Miss Francis reaching for the metronome, when Brenda finally got back to the Music Room. "Sit down quickly, Brenda. Now then - I said sit down, Brenda."

"Please, Miss Francis -"

A look of dire agony appeared on Miss Francis's face - it could have been wind so soon after lunch - and she held the metronome in a strangler's grip.

"I think you've delayed us long enough, Brenda."

"Miss Taylor said couldn't you please excuse me from choir just this once as it's such an important match," said Brenda improvising rapidly, since Miss Taylor had said nothing of the sort. Miss Francis raised a claw.

"I believe I made myself perfectly clear the first time. Now, sit down, please."

"But they're all waiting for me."

"So are we, Brenda. I must remind you that it is not common practice in this school to postpone activities for the sake of Second Year girls. What position do you occupy in the team? First bat?" Miss Francis knew quite well that there are no bats required in a hockey game, but her ignorance suggested that she was above such things.

"Goalkeeper, Miss Francis."

"Goalkeeper? From the fuss certain persons are making, I imagined that you must be at least a fast bowler. Is there no one else in the lower school to rival your undoubted excellence at keeping goal?"

"I did get chosen for the team, Miss Francis."

"Clearly you have no equal, Brenda. That being the case, you hardly need to practise, do you?"

"Miss Taylor thinks I do," said Brenda.

"Well, I'm afraid I don't. I would never, for one moment, keep you from a match, my dear, but practice on a Thursday is an entirely different matter. Sit down."

Brenda, panicking, pointed to the window. "But she won't start without me."

"Neither will I. You may return very quickly and tell Miss Taylor so. At once."

Brenda set off along the corridor, expecting to hear the first notes of "An die Musik" break out behind her. There was only silence. They were still waiting.

"Now run and get changed," said Miss Taylor, swinging her whistle, as Brenda came up the steps again. "We've waited long enough for you, my girl."

"Miss Francis says I can't come," Brenda said, baldly.

"Does she, now?"

"I've got to go back." A scarcely suppressed jeer rose from the rest of the team, assembled in the Changing Room.

"Brenda, this is the Under-Thirteen Eleven, not the Under-Thirteen Ten. There must be at least sixty of you in the choir. Are you really telling me that your absence will be noticed?"

"Miss Francis'll notice it," said Brenda.

"Then she'll just have to notice it," said Miss Taylor under her breath, but loudly enough for Brenda to hear and appreciate. "Go and tell Miss Francis that I insist you attend this practice."

"Couldn't you give me a note, please?" said Brenda. Miss Taylor must know that any message sent via Brenda would be heavily edited before it reached its destination. She could be as insulting as she pleased in a note.

"A note?" Brenda might have suggested a dozen red roses thrown in with it. "I don't see any reason to send a note. Simply tell Miss Francis that on this occasion she must let you go."

Brenda knew that it was impossible to tell Miss Francis that she must do anything, and Miss Taylor knew it too. Brenda put in a final plea for mercy.

"Couldn't you tell her?"

"We've already wasted ten minutes, Brenda, while you make up your mind."

"You needn't wait - "

"When I field a team, I field a team, not ten-elevenths of a team." She turned and addressed the said team. "It seems we'll have to stay here a little longer," her eyes strayed to the Music Room windows, "while Brenda arrives at her momentous decision."

Brenda turned and went down the steps again.

"Hurry UP, girl."

Miss Taylor's huge voice echoed dreadfully round the confining walls. She should have been in the choir herself, singing bass to Miss Humphry's tenor. Brenda began to run and like a cuckoo from a clock, Gill Rogers sprang out of the cloakroom as she cantered past.

"Is that you again?"

Brenda side-stepped briskly and fled towards the Music Room, where she was met by the same ominous silence that had seen her off. The choir, cowed and bowed, crouched over the open music sheets and before them, wearing for some reason her indomitable expression, sat Miss Francis, tense as an overwound clockwork mouse and ready for action.

"At last. Really, Brenda, the suspense may prove too much for me. I thought you were never coming back." She lifted her hands and brought them down sharply on the keys. The choir jerked to attention. An over-eager soprano chimed in and then subsided as Miss Francis raised her hands again and looked round. Brenda was still standing in the doorway.

"Please sit down, Brenda."

Brenda clung to the door-post and looked hopelessly at Miss Francis. She would have gone down on her knees if there had been the slightest chance that Miss Francis would be moved.

"Well?"

"Please, Miss Francis, Miss Taylor says I must go to the practice." She wished devoutly that she were at home where, should rage break out on this scale, someone would have thrown something; the metronome, perhaps, through the window.

Tock...tock...tock...CRASH! Tinkle tinkle.

But Miss Francis was a lady. With tight restraint she closed the lid of the piano.

"It seems," she said, in a bitter little voice, "that we are to have no music today. A hockey game is to take precedence over a choir practice."

"It's not a game," said Brenda. "It's a practice, for a match. Just this once...?" she said, and was disgusted to find a tear boiling up under her eyelid. "Please, Miss Francis."

"No, Brenda. I don't know why we are enduring this ridiculous debate (Neither do I Miss Francis) but I thought I had made myself quite clear the first time you asked. You will not miss a scheduled choir practice for a unscheduled hockey practice. Did you not explain this to Miss Taylor?"

"Yes I did!" Brenda cried. "And she said you wouldn't miss me."

Miss Francis turned all reasonable. "Miss you? But my dear child, of course we wouldn't miss you. No one would miss you. You are not altogether indispensable, are you?"

"No, Miss Francis."

"It's a matter of principle. I would not dream of abstracting a girl from the hockey team, or a netball team or even, heaven preserve us, from a shove-ha'penny team, and by the same token I will not allow other members of staff to disrupt my choir practices. Is that clear?"

What do Miss Taylor and Miss Francis think of each other?

"Yes, Miss Francis."

"Go and tell Miss Taylor. I'm sure she'll see my point."

"Yes. Miss Francis." Brenda turned to leave, praying that the practice would at last begin without her, but the lid of the piano remained shut.

This time the Head Girl was waiting for her and had her head round the cloakroom door before Brenda was fairly on her way down the corridor.

"Why didn't you come back when I called you, just now?"

Brenda leaned against the wall and let the tear escape, followed by two or three others.

"Are you crying because you've broken rules," Gill demanded, "or because you got caught? I'll see you outside the Sixth-Form Room at four o'clock."

"It's not my fault."

"Of course it's your fault. No one forced you to run."

"They're making me," said Brenda, pointing two-handed in either direction, towards the Music Room and the Changing Room.

"I daresay you asked for it," said Gill. "Four o'clock, please," and she went back into the Senior cloakroom in the hope of catching some malefactor fiddling with the locks on the lavatory doors.

This last injustice gave Brenda a jolt that she might otherwise have missed, and the tears of self-pity turned hot with anger. She trudged along to the Changing Room.

"You don't exactly hurry yourself, do you?" said Miss Taylor. "Well?"

"Miss Francis says I can't come to hockey, Miss Taylor."

Miss Taylor looked round at the restive members of the Under-Thirteen XI and knew that for the good of the game it was time to make a stand.

"Very well, Brenda, I must leave it to you to make up your mind. Either you turn out now for the practice or you forfeit your place in the team. Which is it to be?"

What choice will Brenda make?

Brenda looked at Miss Taylor, at the Music Room windows, and back to Miss Taylor.

"If I leave now, can I join again later?"

"Good Lord. Is there no end to this girl's cheek? Certainly not. This is your last chance, Brenda."

It would have to be the choir. She could not bear to hear the singing and never again be part of it, Thursday after Monday, term after term. If you missed a choir practice without permission, you were ejected from the choir. There was no appeal. There would be no permission.

"I'll leave the team, Miss Taylor."

She saw at once that Miss Taylor had not been expecting this. Her healthy face turned an alarming colour, like Lifebuoy kitchen soap.

"Then there's nothing more to say, is there? This will go on your report, you understand. I cannot be bothered with people who don't take things seriously."

She turned her back on Brenda and blew the whistle at last, releasing the pent-up team from the Changing Room. They were followed, Brenda noticed, by Pat Stevens, the reserve who had prudently put on the shin-pads in advance.

Is this the end of the story? What might happen now?

Brenda returned to the Music Room. The lid of the piano was still down and Miss Francis's brittle little elbow pinned it.

"The prodigal returns," she announced to the

choir as Brenda entered, having seen her approach down the corridor. "It is now one fifteen. May we begin dear?"

"Yes, Miss Francis."

"You finally persuaded Miss Taylor to see reason?"

"I told her what you said."

"And?"

"She said I could choose between missing choir practice and leaving the team."

Miss Francis was transformed into an angular little effigy of triumph.

"I see you chose wisely, Brenda."

"Miss Francis?"

"By coming back to the choir."

"No, Miss Francis ..." Brenda began to move towards the door, not trusting herself to come any closer to the piano. "I'm going to miss choir practice. I came back to tell you."

"Then you will leave the choir, Brenda. I hope you understand that."

"Yes, Miss Francis."

> **Did she make the right decision?**
> **How will she feel now?**

She stepped out of the room for the last time and closed the door. After a long while she heard the first notes of the piano, and the choir finally began to sing. Above the muted voices a whistle shrilled, out on the playing-field. Brenda went and sat in the Junior cloakroom, which was forbidden in lunch hour, and cried. There was no rule against that.

1. From reading the first paragraph draw a simple diagram to show the position of the quadrangle, the music room, the changing room, the playing fields and the three characters - Brenda, Miss Taylor and Miss Francis. Using dotted lines perhaps in different colours, trace the journeys Brenda takes between them.

2. By drawing a diagram of Brenda's journeys you will have been thinking about the STRUCTURE of the story i.e. the way it is organised. List the content of all the different conversations Brenda has with the other three characters. You will probably be surprised there are so many. The story is built around these conversations.

3. Place two headings on your sheet, one saying MISS FRANCIS, the other saying MISS TAYLOR. List:
   (a) Phrases which give you an idea of the sort of person each one is.
   (b) Things they say which give you an idea of their character.

4. Have you noticed that Miss Francis is compared to an animal five times? She is compared to a snake, a budgerigar, a stork, a clockwork mouse. She is also described as raising "a claw". How many of these animal references did you include in your list? Find the reference to each animal in the story and explain why the author has described Miss Francis in that way.

5. People are said to be using SARCASM when they make comments which are hurtful, scornful or mocking. Choose three comments made by Miss Francis which you would describe as being sarcastic and copy them out. Practise saying them aloud in the way you think she would have spoken them.

6. Imagine that Miss Francis and Miss Taylor meet the next day. Write out the conversation which they had about the incident. Remember that they will try to be polite to each other.

7. The incident with the Head Girl Gill does not seem to be absolutely necessary, but the story would be weaker without it. Why do you think the author has chosen to include this incident?

REMINDER - Synonyms.

You have been using verbs all the way through this book and you know that whereas nouns **name** people and things, verbs actually tell us what they **do**, e.g. Brenda *cried* at the end of Jan Mark's story.

It is very easy to become boring when you write, if you use the same verbs all the time. English is a language packed with **SYNONYMS** - words of a similar meaning. Think of all the synonyms you can use instead of TO MOVE, e.g. to jump, to run, to gallop, to tumble. Each one is accurate, and can be used much more effectively than a vague verb.

Go back through the story. Does Jan Mark vary her use of verbs to make her writing interesting? Has she made up any new and interesting verbs?

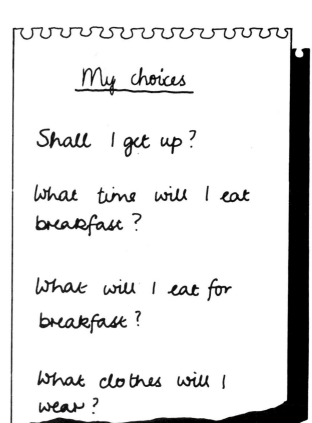

My choices

Shall I get up?

What time will I eat breakfast?

What will I eat for breakfast?

What clothes will I wear?

Now try ......

8 We all make fairly trivial choices every day ("Shall I have toast or cereal for breakfast") but at other times we have to make choices which are more difficult and sometimes choices which are painful. Put the heading CHOICES and make a list of choices different people might have to make. In brackets say who the person is (e.g. young boy, teacher, business man). Phrase the choices in terms of questions as in the example. Remember to use a question mark.
Shall I let my child go on the school camp?
Shall I bring my child on the family holiday we planned? (Parent)

9 Perhaps you can remember a difficult decision you had to make at some time.
Think about the dilemmas you had to face, what kinds of alternatives you had, and why you finally made your decision.

10 Choose one situation and in groups of three act out two scenes showing one person being persuaded to act in two different ways by two different people.

11 Choose a situation involving someone having to make a choice for a story of your own.
Use one of the role play situations if you wish. Follow these steps:
- decide what the choice is going to be
- decide on how many conversations there will be and where they will take place (could be on the telephone)
- make some notes on the type of people your characters will be
- decide on the final outcome (which course of action will be taken. Neither? Both?)
- when you have a clear plan you can concentrate on writing your first draft, making it as lively and interesting as possible.

12.2 Poetry Anthology.

Your task is to assemble a poetry anthology. Following these stages you can work individually or in groups.

(1) Decide whether your anthology will be on a theme (like animals, school) or whether it will be general (Poems I like because .....)

(2) Collect together poems which you like - you will need to search in school books and in the library.

(3) Decide how you are going to present each poem. Will it be written in a shape? Will it be copied on to a black silhouette? Will it be illustrated? Will it have an illuminated first letter? Will it be presented with a decorated border? Can you find or take photographs to go with it? Will you be able to use a typewriter or word processor?

(4) Try to include some poems of your own.

(5) Depending on the poems you have chosen, you might be able to create some interesting effects with some of them. Here are some ideas.
Delete key words in the poem for people to guess what they are.
Write a letter to go with the poem, perhaps to explain the background.
Write a newspaper article to go with the poem, which discusses the central idea.
Invent the story behind the poem.
Change some of the words and include both versions for comparison.
Write some comments on the poem.
Think of some questions to get people thinking about the poem.
Take photographs to go with the poem.

(6) Assemble the poems and illustrations to make the anthology.

A Shadow

Bright light creates a
Stretched
Dark figure
Walking beside you.

A shadow is a soul
Risen from the body
Just cremated by the sun.

No meaning -
Just a haunting
Image.

You can look
But never touch.
It appears -
Then fades
Into the ground.

A creepy ghost.
Company
In an empty room.

Place your hand on the wall.
A hand is placed on your palm.
Your brother lives in a lonely
world of his own.

Jitendra Patel

The ruler

The mathematical aid.
The time saver.
The cheap worker.
The measurement of space.
The dead metre.
The shortest distance.
The fastest runner.
The cleverest competitor.
The most simple machine.
The machine that needs nothing.

Tryfon Gavriel

Bus QQQQqqqqqqqqqq

n Ways of looking at a blackboard

rawled upon aimlessly,
ndlessly battered,

ck as the darkest night?
een as the first spring grass.

neared with the remains of knowledge
recently acquired.

rvous, alone
front of everyone.

eaking round and round,
dlessly punished.

rched on a stand,
aster of its surroundings.

eryone else gone.
smantled, alone, forgotten,

ank, naked, then
oused, degraded,

upid, ignorant, until
ld answers to countless questions
ked by growing minds.

nding on an A
olding every letter.

emy Schryber

The Bat

By day the bat is cousin to the mouse.
He likes the attic of the aging house.

His fingers make a hat about his head.
His pulse beat is so low we think him dead.
He loops in crazy figures half the night.
Among the trees that face the corner light.

But when he brushes up against a screen,
We are afraid of what our eyes have seen:

For something is amiss or out of place
When mice with wings can wear a human face.

Theodore Roethke

Glasses

I wear them. They help me. But I
Don't care for them. Two birds, steel hinges
Haunt each an edge of the small sky
My green eyes make. Rim horn impinges
Upon my vision's furry fringes;
Faint dust collects upon the dry,
Unblinking shield behind which cringes
My naked, deprecated eye.

My glaze feels aimed. It is as if
Two manufactured beams had been
Lodged in my sockets - hollow, stiff,
And gray, like mailing tubes - and when
I pivot, vases topple down
From tabletops, and women frown.

John Updike

Teachers

Wild animals - love a good lunch of literature.
Enjoy chewing an argument.
A loud animal, nocturnal in habit.
Smart, quick, clean.
Not too vicious -
But if provoked, will attack without mercy.

Erel Ahmet

Acknowledgements

The Publishers would like to thank the following authors and publishers for permission to reproduce their material:

The Return of the Antelope by Willis Hall - the author and The Bodley Head.

Faithful Hachiko from *Reading for Adults* by Richard Lewis (1973) - the Longman Group UK.

Tales of Ancient China by Gary Chalk - Century Hutchinson Ltd.

What? by Ivor Cutler - the author and Trigram Press.

Swallows and Amazons by Arthur Ransome - the Arthur Ransome Estate and Jonathan Cape Ltd.

The Shell by James Stephens - The Society of Authors on behalf of Mrs Iris Wise.

Time Out by Robin Chambers, from *The Ice Warrior and Other Stories* - the author and Kestrel Books.

My neighbour Mr Normanton by Charles Causley - Macmillan and David Higham Associates Ltd.

The Lock Out by Colin Thiele - the author and Rigby Publishers (Weldon Publishing of Australia).

My Family and Other Animals by Gerald Durrell - the author and Grafton Books, a division of William Collins Sons and Co Ltd.

Hedgehog by Anthony Thwaite - from *Poems 1953-1988* (Hutchinson, 1989) by permission of the author.

The Wonderful World of Henry Sugar by Roald Dahl - the author and Murray Pollinger.

Geography Lesson by John Fuller - the author.

The Fair to Middling by Arthur Calder-Marshall - the author.

They have yarns by Carl Sandburg - from *The People Yes* by Carl Sandburg, copyright 1936 Harcourt Brace Jovanovich, Inc. and renewed 1964 by Carl Sandburg, reprinted by permission of the publisher.

Foolish Questions by William Cole - the author and Methuen Children's Books.

New English Bible - copyright 1970 by permission of Oxford and Cambridge University Presses.

The Choice is Yours by Jan Mark, from *Nothing to be Afraid Of* - the author and Kestrel Books.

The Bat by Theodore Roethke, from *The Collected Poems of Theodore Roethke* - Faber and Faber.

Glasses by John Updike from *Hoping for Hoopoe* - Victor Gollancz Ltd.

PHOTOGRAPHS

The Publishers would like to acknowledge:
Jonathan Cape Ltd from their catalogue of children's books.
The Brotherton Collection, University of Leeds for the photograph of the Cottingley fairies.
Jan and Jim Crawley for the animal photographs.
Ray Kitching, Eileen Brown and Mike Fleming for other photographs.
The Nissan Company and Wella UK.

ILLUSTRATORS

Eric Jones, Philip Hodgson, Sal Shuel, Paul Bevan, Dandy Palmer, Denby Designs.
Cover design by Tanglewood Graphics, Broadway House, The Broadway, London SW19. Tel: 01 543 3048.
Cover illustration by Abacus Publicity Ltd.

Our thanks to the staff and students of Egglescliffe Comprehensive who have trialled material, and provided examples of students' own work, and to students at Friern Barnet who provided much of the poetry for the Anthology section. Peter Ledwick and students from Tulse Hill school invented The Whopper.

The publishers have made every effort to contact copyright holders but this has not always been possible. If any have been overlooked we will be pleased to make any necessary arrangements.

ANSWERS

Page 5
A = the skin of an orange.
B = a battery
C = a salt-pot
D = a box of matches

Page 38
The message states: "The secret file will be left behind the bench in the park."

Page 54
4, 12 and 16 are false, the rest are true.

Page 55
1 = cautiously
2 = bright
3 = slowly
4 = smoothly
5 = excited